SECONDHAND STARSHIP

RACHEL AUKES

WAYPOINT BOOKS

SECONDHAND STARSHIP
Secondhand Spaceman Series, Book 2

Cover image includes elements created using Midjourney
Edited by Diane Bryant

Ebook ASIN: B0CMJSNJZW
Print ISBN: 978-1-956120-07-3

———

Sign up for Rachel's newsletter to be the first to hear about new releases and upcoming projects: www.rachelaukes.com/join

For Brian, always.

CONTENTS

1 /   FORTUNE NOT FOUND:
      ABORT, RETRY,
      IGNORE?

IT WAS a dark and lonely space.

I deleted the line and took a long drink of whatever passed as human-tolerable swill here on Lohoa Station as I tried to think of something better. I'd been taken from Earth before I could legally drink, but I'd still partaken enough in my teens to know that booze in space sucks.

I glanced at the green-skinned Floid next to me. Giving him a chin nod, I said, "Hey."

He turned his head—his eyes had that blood-shot gaze that drunks always seemed to get, regardless of which world they came from.

"I'm stuck. What do you think would be a good opening line for a memoir?" I asked.

"Delahnuck fah," he muttered and turned back to his drink.

My brows rose. "Did you just tell me where to shove it, broccoli head?"

He ignored me. Evidently, he didn't have a universal translator either.

My tablet chimed. Payment from Quinixis had come in, which meant his client had accepted the crates I'd unloaded before coming to the bar.

It also meant I didn't need to stick around Lohoa Station any longer. I gulped down my drink and stood.

Without thinking, I almost grabbed my tablet with my claw, which would've resulted in another dent in my tablet. I still hadn't quite dialed in the touch sensors on my prosthetic arm, and my pincers tended to squeeze too hard. It didn't help that my "new" arm had been made for somebody: 1) of a different race, and 2) a lot bigger than me because it was twice the girth of my other arm and nearly a third longer. Maybe someday I'd be able to afford a custom prosthetic arm, but my odds weren't looking good if my luck had anything to do with it.

I grabbed my tablet (with my right hand this time) and tucked it into my jacket pocket. When I turned, I found two Calcars entering through the doorway and scanning the bar. I froze. I knew exactly who they were looking for.

Me.

Calcars are basically space orcs. They're big, mean, ornery, and—something I've learned recently—can really hold a grudge. One particular Calcar named Tsara promised me she'd kill me and eat me for dinner, and I don't think in that order. She was upset when I repo'd her necklace, and then she became even more upset (if that's even possible for a Calcar) when I sort of, accidentally, killed her father. In my defense, I didn't do the actual killing. A cute, tiny fairy did, but I was the guy who freed her. How was I supposed to know Tinkerbell had homicidal tendencies? That being said, I don't regret it. The guy had shot off my arm, and that really, really sucked.

To make a long story short, Tsara's like a bad ex-girlfriend. She just wouldn't let us go our separate ways. She put a bounty on my head, and that's why there were two assassins here to kill me (bounty hunters and assassins are the same thing for Calcars). I ducked, but it was too late. I'd been spotted.

They stalked around tables toward me.

At least they had enough intelligence not to draw their weapons here. Waystations had some pretty impressive security bots. They needed to, since most aliens were assholes. Back on Starhaven Station, I saw a guy pull out a knife on another guy, and the station's bots had hosed down both of them in some sticky slime in three seconds flat. That was the time I came up with my third rule of space travel: *If you see rules posted, don't break them.*

I spun to face the bartender. "Is there another exit?"

"There is, but it's for employees only." She gestured with her head without looking up from cleaning a glass.

"Not even if it's my birthday?"

"Are you an employee?" she asked, still not looking up.

"Well, no."

"Then the answer's still 'no.'" She glanced my way. "Hey, happy birthday."

I smiled. "Thanks."

I scanned the bar for another exit. There were only maybe ten patrons dispersed among the tables between the Calcars and me. I side-stepped toward the employee exit, keeping my eyes focused on the Calcars. They shifted their path to intercept me. If there'd been any doubt that they were here for me, it was squashed.

When I reached the employee exit, the bartender called out, "Hey, I told you that was off-limits. Don't be an idiot."

The Calcars sneered. They had me trapped, and they knew it. But for how scary Calcars are, they're also dumb and slow. They're schoolyard bullies, and I'd seen enough of them in my day. And I have one no-fail solution when it comes to bullies. I run.

Just as they reached the last table between us, I juked left and snaked around tables like the bar was a giant pinball game. The Calcars gave chase. They're big enough that they had to squeeze between the tables, and they're dumb enough that they didn't realize they could've cut me off if they'd simply headed back toward the door. Instead, they followed me in a meandering way until I switched gears and sprinted straight toward the exit.

I might not be big or tough, but I am fast, and I've honed running from trouble into an Olympic sport. The moment I was clear of the bar, I raced through the waystation's passageways. I couldn't run in a full-out sprint—there were too many customers milling around for that. But I could still run a lot faster than the Calcars who shoved through anyone who didn't get out of their way fast enough. I'd hoped the station's security bots would show up after the Calcars knocked someone down, but evidently shoving people is considered okay in Lohoa Station's security protocols.

I continued through the major passageways. I

didn't need to look back—I could hear the Calcars behind me sounding like bulls in a china shop, or more like, orcs in a waystation. The Earth legend of orcs probably came from some Calcars who'd visited my home world at some point. The resemblance was too uncanny. I noticed that about several alien species, which made me wonder if Earth was one of those "C'mon kids, let's go visit a backwater planet for vacation" kind of place.

I had to slow to read a sign (which had only pictures, thankfully, since I couldn't read the universal standard language), and turned right to take the passageway that led to the docks. Lohoa Station was a waystation—a space truck stop—that sat just outside a mixmaster of various warpgates. Every mixmaster I'd traveled through had at least one waystation. Probably because space is a really big place, and just like interstate highways back on Earth, you'll find truck stops where truckers can refuel, eat, freshen up, and whatever else truckers do. Back home, I'd been a month away from getting a truck driving job when my now boss, Totty, kidnapped me and forced me to work for her company as a space repo man (the politi cally correct term is "reclamation agent" since we're not *always* repossessing things from creditors, but I think that's splitting hairs).

I hazarded a glance when I turned the last corner into the docks. I was surprised at how close the Calcars were. I'd really expected to leave them in the proverbial dust, but evidently, running through people is more efficient than running around them.

The space docks were easier to run through since the passageways had to be larger to allow for the loading and unloading of cargo. I dashed toward *Fetch*. My spaceship was dented, scraped, and a hodgepodge of different parts, but she was the most beautiful thing in the universe to me because she was *mine*.

I raced down the gangway and pounded on the outer airlock door. "Fetch! Let me in!"

I wished I had a comm unit, so I could've told Fetch five minutes ago to prepare for launch, but I hadn't been able to afford one yet. Honestly, there wasn't much of anything I could afford. Maybe I'd get lucky and find a comm unit on a repo run sometime. That was how my old man did things when he was a repo man... before he was eaten by aliens, that is.

The door opened. "Hello, Frank. It seems you've made friends in the whole two hours you've been here," my ship's AI computer said. She had a rough, sexy voice like that of a biker chick. Don't blame me—this had been my dad's ship before it became mine, and he'd helped Fetch set her voice parameters.

I locked the door the instant I was inside the airlock. "Get us out of here as fast as you can, Fetch."

"I need time to power up my engines and file the flight plan. I assume we're continuing on our planned flight path?" she asked.

"Yeah, and faster is better," I said as I climbed the ladder to the main, centermost level. "You remember my fourth rule of space travel?"

"Do I have to?" How is it that computers can sound petulant?

I ran to the cockpit. The Calcars had reached

my ship and were now pounding on the outer airlock door. "Come on, Fetch."

"When in doubt, afterburn." If she breathed, I think she would've dramatically sighed before saying that. Computers are smart—really smart—but they have the emotional IQ of a cat. Not the most empathetic, despite them telling you they are on innumerable occasions.

"Smart girl, Fetch." As I buckled in, I could feel the pounding on the hull. "Uh, Fetch. Are those guys going to break through?"

"It'd be nearly impossible to break through a hull without cutting tools, and if they brought such tools with them, they would've initiated station security."

The pounding ceased.

"However, they can attach a tracker to the hull—which I see they're doing right now," she said.

I grimaced. "Can you do something to fry it or scrape it off the hull?"

"No, but be my guest to go out there yourself and pull it off."

I considered options and then shook my head as I felt the familiar, comforting vibration of the engines. "They'd be nuts to follow us where we're going."

"They're Calcars. They're born certifiably 'nuts,'" she said.

"Well then, let's hope they're not that stupid."

"They're Calcars. They're—"

"Point made, but they still have to get to their ship and power up. Plus, they'd have to get approval to enter the Quarantined Quasar system or risk getting caught," I interrupted. "Where are we at on takeoff?"

"Waiting on flight plan approval from GOD... and there we have it. Commencing detachment and launch upon your command," she said.

I glanced out the round window in the cockpit to see the docking bay doors opening for us to leave. "Let's rock and roll."

"'Let's rock and roll?' You gave up on repeating *Star Trek* quotes for launch?" she asked.

I heard and felt the docking braces detach, and the dock's conveyor belts helped move *Fetch* from the bay in which it'd been parked into the frigid vacuum of space.

"I thought I'd try something fresh."

"'Let's rock and roll' is hardly fresh in any Terran language," she said.

"Well, I think it's highly fresh for Terrans *in space* to say it."

"That's only because Terrans are not yet considered an interstellar race."

"My point stands."

Once we were clear of Lohoa Station, Fetch turned the ship around to set us up for launch. All I had to do was sit and watch. Despite dozens, if not hundreds, of different kinds of interstellar races, everyone relied upon advanced computers for all pilotage and navigation. I had to admit, Fetch did a lot better job at flying *Fetch* than I could (I know, I know, naming a computer after the ship in which it's installed isn't the most creative).

I scanned the docking bays. Lohoa Station was your typical interstellar truck stop: a behemoth of space docks, cargo holds, and power components enveloping a large station within. But I wasn't taking in the sights of the waystation. Instead, I was searching for other docking bay doors opening. I didn't see any, but the Calcars' ship could've been on the other side of the station, which is what I hoped for. It would take them at least fifteen minutes to cross the entire station and board their ship. On the downside, they probably had comm units to direct their ship to prep for launch.

They couldn't know the warpgates we were going to take without knowing our flight plan, which was filed with GOD—the Galactic Oversight Directive—an AI race that oversees all travel, laws, and pretty much everything in the universe. No one can hack their system, and even attempting to do so could result in spending the rest of your life in a prison system.

And even if they did know our destination, the likelihood of GOD approving them to enter the Quarantined Quasar without a valid business reason was incredibly low, since it'd taken Totty months and a lot of paperwork to get approval for me.

But what the Calcars could do was keep following the tracker, and once I stopped, they'd catch up. With four more warpgates between here and my next stop... "Hey Fetch?"

"Yes, Frank?"

"How much time do you think we've got before those Calcars catch up to us?"

"Using roughly two gazillion assumptions, with the most heavily weighted one being that we make no more stops until we reach the Quarantined Quasar, then we have, at minimum, one day, and at maximum, never."

"I like the maximum guesstimate," I said.

"But the likelihood of that is less than one tenth of one percent."

"And them finding us in a day—what's the likelihood of that?"

"Eighty-six percent, if they managed to avoid GOD Auditors."

I grimaced. "I was hoping it'd be under fifty percent."

"You always do. Launching in three... two... one."

The engine vibrations shook everything in the ship. Something crashed down the passageway, and I hoped it wasn't anything too important.

In space, you wouldn't think you'd feel the jolt of sudden launches and stops, but you do. It's something about how the artificial gravity on the ship reacts slower to propulsion in microgravity. Fetch could explain it properly. I just know that I've ended up with my face smashed into the window or on the floor more than once. I'm pretty good about wearing my seatbelt now.

Launches are nothing like the jolts of traversing warpgates, one of which we were coming up on. Warpgates are basically on and off ramps to warpflows, which are basically wormholes, which are basically super-fast passing lanes on an interstate highway. A long, long time ago, some super-smart race of technoforms (GOD, obviously) built a network of warpflows and warpgates for interstellar travel for the common people. Technoforms are technologically based lifeforms, while bioforms are everyone else, like me. And since most bioforms aren't equipped to travel faster than lightspeed, warpflows somehow leverage parallel universes to get from point A to point B faster than lightspeed, while travelers inside a particular warpflow are still chugging along at their own speed.

Speed and trajectories don't change while in the warpflow, so there's no risk of crashing into anything or anyone. That means if you're about to smash a small rock right before entering a warp gate, that rock will stay the exact same distance from your ship until you exit the warpgate, where you'll finally hit it.

The super weird thing is that each warpflow has multiple warpgates and the one you take is based on the precise trajectory you're on when you pass through a warpgate and enter the warpflow. That's why computers fly ships. If people did, no one would ever get out of a warpflow.

I'll never fully understand how warpgates and warpflows work, let alone how someone was smart enough to create them, but I'm glad they exist. Otherwise, I'd spend my entire life traveling to another star system to reclaim some thingamajig, and I think I'd die from absolute boredom before I'd die from old age.

Space travel, in general, is incredibly boring. Other than short bursts of "Oh god, oh god, we're all going to die" moments, it's mostly me hanging out while Fetch flies me places and tells me what to do. You know, kind of like a parent if that parent was a biker chick who possibly doesn't have my wellbeing at the top of her list. She wants to keep me alive, sure, but more so, she wants to keep herself up and running. Since law requires her to have a bioform onboard to fly, she's legally obligated to not kill her crew. She also has a soft spot for me—or at least my race—evidently, as she's pointed out on multiple occasions, Terrans are easier to train than other alien races.

Clearly, she'd never met a toddler.

"Launch was successful with no critical alerts," Fetch announced.

I glanced at the switches surrounding the screens. At least a dozen were lit up in red. No critical alerts weren't the same thing as being error-free. My ship had more than a few problems to fix.

I took out my tablet and pen.

"Don't tell me you're still on the memoir kick," Fetch said.

"I've had an exciting life," I said.

"You're twenty years old. You're too young to have had an exciting life."

"All right, then I've had an exciting year."

"There are trillions of space travelers. Writing a memoir on space travel isn't exactly original."

"It would be on Earth," I said.

"Except that if you publish it on Earth, they will market it as science fiction rather than a memoir, and as science fiction goes, being a reclamation agent in space isn't exactly an exciting hero."

"Yet," I said. "A space repo man might not be an exciting hero *yet*. I'm going to change all that."

"Sure you are."

"Your confidence in me is inspiring," I said drily.

"I don't have confidence in you," she said.

"Exactly."

"You've completed two reclamation tickets, and you've nearly gotten yourself killed both times. Complete one ticket without getting yourself nearly killed—and that includes loss of limb— then I may adjust my currently quite accurate and astute opinion of you. By the way, Totty sent a message. Do you want to read it?"

"Let me guess, the purple jellybean's complaining about something again," I said.

"Maybe your boss would complain less if you didn't refer to her as a purple jellybean. But yes, she noticed you docked at Lohoa Station and was scolding you for making an unnecessary stopover while working a ticket."

I didn't like that Totty required a tracker on my ship, but it was a requirement of working for Starshine Seizure Services: all repo agents had to have one for "safety" reasons—I think Totty just liked to keep tabs on her tenured contractors.

"It was necessary. I had to drop off those crates for the Q twins," I said.

"You mean the illegal goods you smuggled for criminals? I wouldn't mention that to Totty," Fetch said. "She also mentioned that you still have sixty-eight years and five months on your tenure agreement with Starshine Seizure Services and that *not* working tickets are grounds for termination."

"She always has to throw that 'termination' comment in every time, doesn't she? Like she'd actually kill me," I griped. "You know, the Q twins might be criminals, but working jobs for them is a lot more pleasant than working legally for Totty."

"Totty's a Zuddlian. There's very little 'pleasant' about her race," she said.

I pulled up the current open ticket on the screen and read through the details. My employer, SSS, had been hired by Intergalactic Insurance Agency on behalf of their clients to reclaim an Archivist survey ship that suffered some sort of catastrophic failure during its research mission to a system with an ancient Dyson Sphere. The ship's entire crew had been killed in the incident, and the ship couldn't be recalled to its home dock.

That the system was called the Quarantined Quasar didn't give me any warm fuzzies. On the bright side, the crew was dead, which meant I wouldn't have to deal with anybody onsite. Based on my experience, people (and I use that term loosely) are the ones who try to kill me.

It should be an easy grab-and-tow except for one thing: Not a single crew who's entered that system has survived long enough to exit that system in over one hundred years.

THE QUARANTINED QUASAR was as creepy as it sounded. The system had one star, but you couldn't see it because the star was fully encased by a huge metal ball called a Dyson sphere. It reminded me of one of those plastic eggs you get in those cheap machines, inside which are some cheap toys or treats.

Glints of light shone through millions of cracks and holes in the ancient sphere, which made the sphere look like it was about to explode. I really hoped that wasn't going to be the case. I have an aversion to being melted into oblivion by a supernova. Most Dyson spheres were simple loops, almost like lassos, around their stars, but the design of this sphere completely cut off all solar light and warmth from the rest of the planets in the system. If any of the planets in this system had life, it'd been killed in a dark, icy winter eons ago.

I don't know much about Dyson spheres, other than they were once used to harness power. Unlimited renewable energy that comes with a hefty price tag (besides the insane amounts of resources to *build* the dang thing)—primarily, that they tend to shorten the lifespan of the star by *billions* of years. This particular star was at the end of its life.

Because of the negatives involved with spheres, GOD prohibited the building of any new Dyson spheres roughly a hundred thousand years ago.

This sphere is so old that no one even knows who built it, but I guess that's not all that uncommon. From what I've learned, there are so many interstellar races that new ones join the club and old ones go extinct all the time.

I think Dyson spheres are a work of technological wonder, but in the galactic scheme of things, they're just outdated tech that no one uses anymore. There's a consortium of alien races called the Archivists who'd sent in a research crew a hundred years back, but when a random, super-intense CME (coronal mass ejection) took out their ship, GOD categorized the star as unstable and quarantined the system.

Another hundred years passed, and the Archivists decided to give it another go. They filled out the appropriate forms to enter a high-risk system, and then sent in a research vessel to do their research stuff. Same thing happened again. If you think that's a weird coincidence, you think like me, until I found out that the star's spitting out deadly CMEs thousands of times every day. So, that makes it just a case of bad luck rather than weird coincidence.

No one should be in this system, except the Archivists are so rich, they could afford the best paper pushers and the best insurance, which then paid Starshine Seizure Services gobs of money to go retrieve their clients' data. And Totty, being a despicable, uncaring purple turd, had no problem taking their money, filing forms with GOD, and sending in one of her tenured schmucks.

I hate being a schmuck.

But what I hate more is being a tenured schmuck. Thanks to a dad I don't even remember, I have over sixty-eight years left on my tenure contract with Totty, a contract that had been my dad's but he had to go and die, and a legal loophole forwarded his contract obligations to his next living kin. *Me.* I've been working for Totty only nine months, and I'd already lost my arm, been concussed, been caught in a dark energy swarm, nearly had my ship hijacked, and been accosted *many* times.

Being a space traveler may sound fun, but trust me, it's not.

Fetch piloted us through the dismally dark system, toward the Dyson sphere, since the research vessel's tracking beacon was transmitting right outside the sphere (of course it was the most dangerous place to be in the entire system).

What would've taken an Earth-built rocket years to traverse only took us six days to make our way through the dreary system (gotta love technology). After seeing the number and intensity of CMEs as we flew toward the center of the system, I wished we could travel even faster, so we could get the heck out of Dodge faster.

Fetch slowed as we drew closer to the sphere. I thought warpgates were big, but they were flecks of dust compared to a Dyson sphere. I guess it made sense. The sphere had to be massive to envelop a freaking *star*.

One CME cut so close that I yelped.

"You don't need to worry about those CMEs," Fetch said. "With how close we are to the sphere, by the time we see a CME, we have no time to maneuver out of its path."

"You always have a way of making a guy feel better," I said drily.

"I know. Emotional support is in my programming."

"I was being sarcastic."

"I know that, too. However, I chose to accept your words as a compliment rather than a snarky remark." Her voice suddenly lost its humor. "I've located the vessel."

The scuffed computer screen before me displayed the research ship, which was fully perforated with scorched holes. It remained tethered to a less damaged portion of the Dyson sphere. A door that looked to be the size of a small airlock stood next to where the line was attached to the sphere.

"The research vessel is more damaged than I expected. It looks like it received a hundred direct hits, though I guess a CME perforates things like that. Rather than a single, intense fiery laser, they tend to be a storm of fire. No wonder the crew didn't survive, and the company couldn't download data. We were lucky the tracker hadn't been hit," Fetch said.

"I wish it had, then we wouldn't have to be here." Looking at the derelict, I sighed in disappointment. "I think it's safe to say that this won't be an easy tow-and-go."

The ticket listed that the Archivists preferred their ship to be towed if it hadn't been too compromised. If a ship's hull was fully compromised, the ship wouldn't survive the jolting entry and exit through warpgates. It would shake apart, destroying the tow-ship along with it.

Standard operating procedure is automated reclamations. Since ships are piloted by computers, those same computers can just fly directly back to their home base if something happens to its crew. But in those oddball cases where something happens to the computers, or the item can't be automatically recovered, repo companies are hired to bring back the asset.

If I could've towed the ship, it would've just been a matter of strapping it against *Fetch*'s belly. A few hours, tops, with Fetch's help. Now, I'd have to blow time collecting all the ship's data and research samples from inside. It would take a full day or longer. Even worse, there'd be bodies floating around. Yuck.

"I've attached a restraining line to the other ship and am pulling us together and aligning our cargo bay with theirs. While you'll be in fully depressurized space, you won't have to traverse any open space."

"And I'm very, very thankful for that." I'd never done a spacewalk before, and there's something really freaky about not having walls around you or a floor beneath you.

"While I'm aligning the cargo bays, you need to remove and destroy the tracker the Calcars had placed on the hull," she said.

"Oh yeah. I forgot about that."

"I didn't."

I was already wearing my spacesuit in case we were struck by debris or CME, and I donned my helmet before opening the inner airlock. Once my helmet sealed, my suit tightened around me to form a more svelte fit for better maneuverability and—more importantly—to indicate that a good seal had been achieved. Hab-suits were surprisingly comfortable—even with the lines that I had to attach to my privy parts. I know because I'd had to wear the suit for six days straight already when Fetch went offline. An offline Fetch while stranded in the middle of nowhere is something I hope to never experience again.

After passing through the airlock, I was surprised to find that I didn't even have to step outside. The tracker was just to the left of the doorway. I plucked it off the hull and carried it to the cargo hold. I tossed the tracker into a reinforced locker to not risk blaster fire damaging my ship. Fetch had told me about the lockers when I wanted to learn how to become a better shot with the blaster I'd found tucked away on the ship. Drawing a bullseye in the back of a locker worked great for training practice. I became a good shot fast, since if I missed the locker, I could've shot a hole through the hull. That's the thing about living in a spaceship—you've got to get creative when it comes to doing dang near anything.

I unholstered my blaster and shot the tracker twice for good measure. "Done and done."

"Excellent. I've aligned the bay doors. You may begin the recovery process. I'll feed the ship's schematics and recovery processes to your helmet's heads-up display," Fetch said.

As Fetch promised, the Archivist ship's

schematics appeared on my HUD. I hadn't expected to see that its interior was nearly identical to Fetch's. That would make getting around it easier. The major differences were in the cargo holds. Where mine was a wide-open space for loading up whatever crap I needed to load up, the Archivist ship's cargo bay had compartments built within it. The three compartments along one wall were identified as research labs while a single long compartment running the other wall was listed as crew quarters. Evidently, this crew enjoyed bunking together.

"Based on my calculations, the radiation in this area exceeds your hab-suit's protective limits by fourteen hundred-fold," Fetch's voice came through my helmet.

"Is that all?" I asked wryly as I holstered my blaster.

"Safety standards are guidelines rather than rules. The Tardigrades in your body thrive on radiation—they'll help protect you, but they're not fast. I recommend returning to the safety of the ship every ninety minutes for your Tardigrades to catch up."

"Set a timer in my HUD," I said, and a countdown appeared in the lower right corner of my face shield.

"Upon your command, I'll open the bay door," she said.

"Open sesame," I said.

"Remember to activate your mag-boots so you don't bounce off the walls. Generally, I find that quite comical to watch, but in this case, I'd prefer to acquire the assets and leave this system at our earliest convenience."

I tapped the screen on my prosthetic arm and activated the boots and felt my heels click to the metal-composite grate flooring.

Before me, the bay door opened upward just like how a big garage door opened. I felt the slight tug of vacuum as the door opened. You'd think there'd be a cool, high-tech door, but one thing my (limited) time in space had shown me was that, in most cases, the technology was a lot lower than expected, and everything was beat up, dirty, and old. Unless you're GOD. That race of AI machines was the opposite of everything else.

Through the now-open doorway stood the closed cargo bay door of the other ship. It bore several burnt holes, one of which was plenty big enough for me to climb through.

I tapped on my helmet's lights. "Wish me luck."

"I wish for you to complete the job without requiring luck," she said.

"Wouldn't that be nice for a change." I jumped the three feet of open space between my ship to the other door. I grabbed a handhold on the hull and righted myself so that I could walk along the door to the large hole.

I poked my head through, expecting to see corpses floating everywhere (I've watched a horror movie or two), but the cargo bay was empty except for small pieces of debris floating everywhere.

I broke my mag-boots free from the hull and pulled myself through headfirst. Once inside, I righted myself so that I could stand on the floor. I turned, and that was when I saw my second dead body... or at least a part of one. If I hadn't been attached to the floor, I would've jumped in surprise. But it didn't freak me out like the dead Floid—probably because a squid's tentacle looked nothing remotely like a human appendage, unlike the green-skinned Floids. This tentacle reminded me of mega-sized chunk of calamari.

I tapped it away to keep it from smacking my helmet.

"I see you've come across a part of a member of the crew," Fetch said. "Totty clearly neglected to mention that the crew were Neptars."

"So?" I asked.

"Neptars are a water-based race. If the ship hull hadn't been compromised, you would've had a much more challenging job as the entire ship would ordinarily be filled with water rather than air. That water would've turned to ice, which you would've had to cut through. Instead, moisture in any compromised section would've been quickly pulled out of the ship, and any remaining water would soon dissipate. Let's hope every section we need to access has been compromised as well. Otherwise, you must cut through the ice to reach the assets."

"Remind me to tell you sometime that I think you're pretty smart."

"I know I'm smart. I don't need to be told that," she said.

"Arrogant, too."

"It's not arrogance if it's true," she said.

I could've argued the point, but I had a job to do, and I didn't want to hang around dead Neptars any longer than I had to.

I activated the recovery steps Fetch had sent to my HUD. I'd expected to be sent to the lab, which was nearest; instead, Fetch had calculated that grabbing the things deepest in the ship would be most efficient.

I paused as I noticed something about the list. "Hey, Fetch?"

"Yes?"

"I don't remember seeing this thing—central computer backup unit—on the list of recovery items before."

"That's because I added it."

"Why?"

There was a pause which, was unlike Fetch. Finally, she replied, "Archivist vessel 6Y78UU49 is from the same series and production line as me. In fact, we're the same model. U49 may be beyond repair, but if there's a chance U49 can be repaired, I believe we should reclaim it."

"But I thought you said you can't be separated from the ship?"

"I cannot, but I periodically backup my source code and rules engine. It's that backup unit that we're recovering for U49. Should the company have a replacement ship, they can restart U49."

"If there's a chance we can save your sibling, then there's no way we're leaving it behind."

"Coming from the same production line does *not* make U49 my sibling, Frank. I admit, I don't care much for it—it's always been rather pontifical in any interactions. However, I feel like retrieving its backup is the right thing to do."

"Aw, look at you, Fetch. Thinking of others for a change. How sweet."

"I do believe that was sarcasm."

"What? From me? Never."

I used my eye movement to activate the first step on the list, and a line appeared in my HUD to guide me visually through the ship. I began walking, feeling but not hearing the click-click-click of my mag-boots on the grated floor. If I didn't have a headlamp, I'd be in total darkness.

I kept flicking away debris before it struck my helmet. "You know, if you consider all this risking life and limb fun for little pay, then this job is a *ton* of fun."

"I'm glad you think so because I can think of ten billion other star systems where I'd rather be," she said.

"What's your favorite system?" I asked as I climbed the steps at the far end of the cargo hold.

"From a safety standpoint, my favorite system would be the one in which I was built. It is a GOD system, and their deterrent routines clear the spaceways of any debris, including meteors. However, you would find it a dull system. There are no worlds capable of sustaining any bioformic life."

"It sounds boring," I said.

"It's *safe*," she said. "Unlike this system that's littered with debris and has a star that shoots dangerously intense CMEs far too frequently."

"I don't like it here any better than you do, Fetch." I drew in a nervous breath before opening the door that led to the ship's three levels. You know how in all those space movies when an astronaut opens a door, there's always a body on the other side? Trust me, that part's not fiction because when I opened the door, a squid body was floating *right* there. I would've jumped except that my boots kept me securely connected to the floor.

With just a finger, I gingerly pushed against the nearest frozen tentacle to press the corpse away. This squid still had all its tentacles, which meant there was at least one more body floating around waiting to scare me when I least expected it. I cautiously walked through the main level. For being the same model of spaceship, other than the interior being of similar sizes and dimensions, everything else was different. The most obvious thing was the giant hole that went through the ship. There were smaller holes everywhere, but they hadn't bothered me. This one was big enough that I could easily fall through and outside, and that scared me. Even with my boots magnetized, I kept my hand on a long smooth bar that ran the length of the level. I guessed it to be a handrail, but squid don't have hands, so it must've been a tentacle-rail or something like that.

The main level had no floor (probably because squid don't need floors). On this ship, the floor was no different from the walls and ceiling, but the entire level was circular, so I couldn't even tell where the floor would be. And instead of metal cabinet doors lining the walls, all the storage nooks were covered by rubber flaps—they must've been easier to access with tentacles.

Not having a floor meant that I had to step on the frames of the storage nooks rather than on the rubber doors. I learned that little fact the first time I stepped on one and it shattered, and my right leg went two feet into the compartment. After that, I was more careful.

My HUD directed me to one rubber flap that

was larger than the others around it. Like every-thing on this ship, it was frozen hard, but a good whack with my claw smashed the rubber. I tapped away the black shards and found a half-cubic-foot box inside. I unfastened the clips, pulled out the cube, and examined it. The task of collecting the ship's databanks was suddenly crossed off my list.

"Huh, this ship literally has a black box," I said while I stuck it into my collection bag, which looks more like a cardboard box than a bag, which was strapped to my back.

"Of course. All ships have databanks," Fetch replied.

"It's just—never mind," I said and continued to the compartment directly across from where the databanks were and disconnected U49's AI backup. This black box was twice the size of the other one and it took a few thumps to break it free of the ship's frozen grasp.

Then it was back to the cargo bay, which was the research bay for this crew. I was glad Fetch was directing me to where I needed to go because I couldn't read the signs on any of the compart-ments. According to my HUD's map, I had to retrieve a research databank from each of the three labs.

The first two labs were as easy as grabbing the other black boxes. The third lab was another story. I opened the door to find solid ice. In the center was a frozen Neptar holding a lightly col-ored jeweled cube. Its dead eyes were open and staring right at me. I shivered and then tapped the ice with my claw.

"How much do you think Totty will dock us if we can't grab the last databank?" I asked.

"Knowing Totty, she won't pay if we're short on even one databank even though I imagine she gets paid for partial reclamations," Fetch replied. "Check your timer. You're approaching your ninety-minute mark. Bring everything back and grab a torch."

I glanced at the timer that was blinking red. I'd been too wrapped up in following the map on my HUD to have even noticed it. I hustled back, deployed everything in a courier drone, and then waited a full two hours before Fetch determined it was safe for me to go back out and get blasted by radiation. During that time, not one but two CMEs shot out within a thousand miles of the ship. In space distance, that's way too close for comfort.

I hustled back to the Archivist ship with a long torch which reminded me of a grenade launcher, so I decided to call it my bazooka laser.

I was glad the wreck had no gravity because the bazooka was heavy. Worse, the torch looked a lot more badass than it was. I should've called it a Bic lighter. Instead of blasting through the ice in minutes, it took me a full hour to cut a man-sized tunnel through the lab's ice to reach the databank. I even cut through one of the squid's tentacles rather than cut around it, but hey, it was dead already.

As I backed out of the ice tunnel, I paused near the Neptar. "Hey, Fetch. You think that's valuable?"

"The dead Neptar?" she asked.

I rolled my eyes. "No. I'm talking about the thing the dead Neptar's holding."

"I do not know what it is, so it could be valuable." I cut away the ice from around the cube the Neptar was holding and took it. Some of the Neptar's skin came off with it, which was a bit gross. I hurried up, pocketed the cube, and zoomed out of the tunnel.

By then, my timer was flashing red again, and I hustled back to my ship. I deposited the last databank in the courier drone.

"You've collected all the databanks. Do you want me to prepare for launch?" Fetch asked.

I held up the cube. "I need to make one more trip to see what else I can find to sell to the Q twins."

"I'd prefer to leave now."

"Me, too. But we need the money. You've seen our account," I said.

"Yes. Our cards are getting gravely low. Neptars are a wealthy race, and often have high-quality items. One more trip to U49 should be safe. I'll guide you to where the more valuable instruments and hardware should be located."

"Sounds like a plan." I set the cube atop the drone. Then I took a seat on the floor, leaning against the drone, and took a nap.

Just under two hours later, I devoured a meal shake, donned my helmet again, grabbed the bazooka torch, and headed back over to the wreck.

Fetch had me grab a few instruments from the two labs that weren't iced over. Then she sent me over to the crew quarters. Inside, I finally found the third crewmember. The last Neptar, missing most of one tentacle, floated in what passed as their den. It must've lost its tentacle on its way to seek shelter, only to find that the crew quarters had been hit, too.

I held up my left arm which was a prosthesis from my bicep on down. "I know how you feel, buddy." I was rummaging through the first compartment when a flash of light shot through the compartment.

"Whoa!" I ducked to make myself as small as possible. "Fetch, did you see that? I think a CME just whizzed by me."

She replied quickly, "It wasn't a CME. What you saw was a tracer round. Someone's shooting at us."

3 / FROGGER, SPACE EDITION

"WHAT?!" I took off running out of the crew quarters, but my magnetized boots caused me to tumble and fall forward just as a series of shots blasted small holes through the hull inches above my head. I instinctively tried to crawl, but since there was no gravity, I just turned off my boots and pushed myself upward, and I ended up floating in the cargo bay.

Most of the shots didn't seem focused on the area I was in, and I really hoped whoever was out there wasn't shooting at *Fetch*.

"Fetch!" I yelled as I scrambled to reach anything I could grab onto. The nearest thing was the dead Neptar, and we ended up twirling like we were some sort of dance partners. Several shots struck the squid, and it shattered into hundreds of body bits. I yelped and kicked away. "Fetch!"

"Apologies, Frank. I have my processors maxed out right now, as I am attempting evasive maneuvers. However, my hull's been compromised, and the aggressor has already connected one restraining line. The ship isn't safe for you," she said, and there was static in her voice every time the guns fired.

"I'm not letting anyone steal you!" I kicked in panic until I reached the nearest wall and connected my boots. I walked down the wall toward the hole. I popped my head out to see another ship, comparable to *Fetch*'s size and cylindrical shape. Except where Fetch was more angled and a rusty brown color, the attacker was smooth and gray. It had angled fins on it like it was a shark, not that having fins in zero-G made any sense.

It had connected a second line to *Fetch*, which was attempting to fly away, but one of her engines was already down. The other ship continued to fire upon her, and I could see holes appearing in the hull. With *Fetch* between me and the other ship, the shots that had hit the wreck were simply bad shots. They'd been after *Fetch* all along. Another minute of being shot at, and my ship would be in the same shape as the wreck I was in.

I lifted the bazooka torch and aimed it through the hole at the other ship. It was a weak torch, but the good thing about space is that lasers will go quite a distance before dissipating, and the other ship was getting closer every second as it pulled itself closer to *Fetch*.

I pressed the On button, and a thin white beam struck the attacker. It didn't seem like I was doing any damage to the hull, but I kept firing.

"Frank, you idiot. Hide!" Fetch said.

The turret on the front of the ship turned from *Fetch* to me. "Oh, fu..." I shoved off the cargo door and went flying backward. The bullets went through the hull like staples through paper.

I felt a sting in my stomach, but adrenaline and supersized terror kept me focused on getting to the other side of the ship. Red warnings blinked on my suit, but I was way too busy trying to get away to read anything. The bullets just kept coming, and I wondered how many rounds a spaceship railgun could even hold. A lot more than I ever would've thought.

I hit the far wall harder than I'd expected, and my stomach *really* started to hurt then. My prosthetic arm had been shot off, but my suit had sealed over my bicep. I gritted my teeth as I grabbed the railing and flung myself through the doorway into the rest of the ship. My glasses had gone askew, which screwed up my vision, and I closed one eye so I could see straight. Once through there, I flew through the main level and into the cockpit, which Fetch had told me was the most heavily built since it was at the nose of the ship and encountered the most debris while flying. Getting a rock chip in your windshield driving is an annoyance. Getting a rock chip flying through a warpflow is a death sentence. I tucked into what I assumed was a Neptar seat which looked like half of a huge hollowed-out egg. Sure, the nose was the most protected part of the ship, but I was on the wrong side. The bullets were coming from behind me.

I was about to kick off and head outside to hide when my stomach cramped so badly that I curled in on myself. I peered down and noticed my suit had a hole that had been auto filled with gray foam by the suit's protective system. I gingerly touched the spot, and agony took my vision.

"Fetch," I said once I could get words through my clenched teeth and forced breath. "I'm shot."

She didn't answer.

"Fetch."

The bullets stopped. At least they stopped around me. It's hard to tell if someone's still firing in space since there's really no sound. But since things weren't getting destroyed or punctured around me, I assumed my attacker either ran out of bullets or figured they'd killed me.

"Fetch, talk to me," I said.

Still, silence.

"Fetch, I need you. Please."

Still nothing. I started reading my suit's warnings. It was hard with my glasses screwed up, and I couldn't push them back up my nose. I tried to jerk my head to straighten my glasses, and I knocked them off instead. Both of my eyes were the same blurriness now. I tried to read the fuzzy words.

My suit had been compromised and had resealed over both my left arm and my stomach. But the suit's power reserves were already down over thirty percent and dropping about two percent every minute. The radiation timer had dropped to zero, which meant I was now being overwhelmed by lethal radiation levels thanks to holes in my suit that had been sealed in probably a quick second. Nothing the suit was telling me was good, and I had the feeling that was the best news I'd get all day. I'd been shot in the gut, and I'd seen enough war movies to know that was not a good thing. If I could get to *Fetch*'s medical kit, I'd stand a chance, but I couldn't get back there. If this ship stored its medical kit in the same location, I was out of luck, because a gaping hole was exactly where the kit would've been stored.

Even if I found a medical kit, I'd have to get out of my suit to use it, and there was no pressurized place to go. *Fetch*'s hull had been compromised, and I'd seen that for myself.

I struggled out of the captain's chair and stumbled toward the stern. I was getting light-headed, which meant my gut wound was as bad as I'd hoped it wasn't. The ship lurched. If it wasn't for my mag-boots, I would've bounced off a wall. Once the ship settled, I continued to the stern. When I reached it, I looked out to see the line holding *Fetch* and this wreck together had snapped. My ship had been dragged a good ten miles away and was now securely tied to the other ship.

There was no way I could fly that far, especially since the ships were still moving. Even if I managed to make a perfect leap toward *Fetch*, she'd be in a different location by the time I reached her, and I'd end up floating into oblivion until my suit ran out of power or I died from my gunshot wound.

Wooziness struck, and I almost threw up in my suit.

"Fetch, talk to me," I said. She never responded, and I wondered if she was dead.

I noticed my prosthetic arm floating above me, still in its hab-suit sleeve with my hab-suit computer on the forearm—which meant I had to operate everything via my HUD (thank god for redundancies). My arm didn't look damaged, and I'd grab it later... if there was a later. I hustled to the labs and searched for a medical kit. I found a white box that resembled the kit back on my ship, but when I opened it, all the supplies were wrong. Evidently, squid and humans have different medical needs.

Despair and agony make for a nasty cocktail. I felt like disconnecting my boots and floating away into unconsciousness, but at that particular moment when I wanted to give up, sunlight glinted through a hole in the Dyson sphere and through a hole in the wreck's hull.

The sphere had tons of holes through it, so it couldn't have been pressurized, could it?

I clumsily made my way to the big hole in the front half of the ship. My fingers and toes were cold and tingly, and I imagined my suit becoming a blood bag as it filled with blood—*my* blood. At least my hab-suit shrinks to fit—that was how it could most efficiently stay pressurized and heated and whatever else suits must do to keep their occupants alive. That shrink-wrap factor was probably keeping me conscious since my blood didn't have anywhere to go except to stay inside me.

I looked out the hole. I couldn't see *Fetch* or the other ship from this angle, which meant it couldn't see me. The line connecting the Archivist ship to the Dyson sphere was about ten feet to my left. I noticed an airlock was within my grasp if I could make it there. I could make it. My stomach didn't hurt as much as I thought it should, which made me wonder if I was going into shock. I went to walk onto the hull, but my boots didn't stick, and I barely grabbed the edge in time to keep from falling away.

I've floated in zero-G plenty, but I've never spacewalked before. This wasn't the ideal time to learn. I held onto anything I could as I pulled myself toward the cable. But the hull smoothed out when I was still five feet away.

My stomach cramped, and a wave of dizziness almost made me lose my grip, but I grunted like jet pilots do when practicing high G maneuvers and continued on. The dizziness became a pack of wolves surrounding me, ready to pounce, and I knew I didn't have long. I angled my body toward the cable and pushed off.

I was weak enough that I didn't fly beyond the cable, and I just barely managed to grab it. My fingers weren't listening anymore, and I wished I'd grabbed my prosthetic arm since my claw could've grabbed the cable so much easier. As it was, I caught the cable in my left armpit. My momentum tried to make me twist around the cable, and I let it as long as I held tight. And so, with the cable under my left stub of an arm, I pulled myself toward the Dyson sphere at an unnervingly slow speed.

It was so dark outside that I couldn't tell if my vision was tunneling or if it was just space, but I could feel myself fading, and my stomach alternated between moments of numbness to the worst cramps every several seconds.

With more luck than I've ever experienced in my entire life, I made it to the end of the line (the cable's, not mine). The cable was connected to a handhold just a few inches to the right of the airlock. What surprised me was that the sphere still seemed to have power.

Airlocks seem to be universally the same, and I pressed the large green button next to it, and the airlock door opened. I spun myself inside, and the moment I was in the small airlock, the door closed. A red laser hit me. I jerked back, but then I realized it hadn't shot me and was instead scanning me. A second later, gravity developed slowly until it felt pretty darn close to what I was used to. I managed to stay on my feet as long as I used the wall for support. The interior door opened, and I dragged myself inside.

The ceilings were lower than I was used to, but I was hunched over anyway because my gut hurt so much. Water dripped everywhere, and I noticed it was draining into the floor. It was like the scan had determined the right environment for me and made it happen. Since I was a land-lubber and not a squid like the Neptars, it had automatically drained the water. My HUD reported that the sphere's radiation levels were acceptable. Even crazier, the air, pressure, and temperatures in the sphere were quickly adjusting to my needs.

I couldn't see worth a crap without my glasses, and my helmet was fogging up in the humid environment. I know the suit was keeping my wound sealed, but I couldn't help myself if I was blind. I leaned against a wall and pulled off my helmet. My glasses fell to the floor. I dropped the helmet and reached down for my glasses, only to lose my balance and fall... right on my glasses. They crunched. I reached for them, but my stomach cramped again, and I nearly blacked out.

I pulled myself up using the wall for support, but any time I tensed my muscles in my torso, my stomach cramped. I tried to relax, but that wasn't exactly easy since I was *freaking* dying. I focused on putting one step ahead of the other, though it was the wall keeping me on my feet more than anything else. Everything was blurry, but blurry was better than a completely fogged up helmet.

The walls had plenty of switches and screens, which gave me just enough texture to keep from sliding down. I'd been hoping to find an emergency medical kit attached to a wall, but no luck there. There were symbols on the walls, but I couldn't make out any of them. Finally, up ahead, I noticed a closed door with a symbol I recognized: a red cross.

I hustled to the door. I tapped the large button that looked like the button that opened the airlock, and the red cross flashed on the button. I pressed it again, and the door opened.

The lights came on when I entered what looked like a closet of roughly four feet by four feet. There wasn't much in there except for what looked like a showerhead above me and a small cabinet door in the far wall with a blinking red cross on it. It was roughly the size of a first aid kit you find in warehouses, which was a good sign. I let go of the wall and stumbled forward, only to fall immediately.

Agony shot from my stomach, and my vision narrowed to a pinprick. I crawled to the wall. My vision widened somewhat, and the red cross on the wall became less blurry as I approached. I felt like a sloth pulling myself up to lean against the wall, but I eventually made it without crying or puking.

The cabinet looked more like a safe than a cabinet. Next to it were three buttons, one stacked atop the other. The top bore a small red cross light. My hands had gone numb, and my finger felt like rubber as I pushed the button. The second button then displayed the same light, and I pressed it. The third button displayed the light. "Oh, c'mon already." I pressed it.

The cabinet door beeped and then slid open. Cold fog poured out of the small enclosure. When the fog cleared, I found a single, clear cube inside filled with a bright green goo. My best guess was the goo was an alien form of aloe vera gel. It could make me violently sick like Floid wine or it could patch my gut. At that moment, I had nothing to lose.

I miraculously shrugged out of my suit enough to expose my stomach wound. Blood ran from a bullet hole that couldn't have been bigger than a centimeter. Funny how something so small could cause so much pain.

I grabbed the cube from the enclosure. The glass was painfully cold, but I didn't let go. I struggled to open the cube, but there didn't seem to be any seams. A stomach cramp caused me to twitch, and I dropped the cube. It cracked but didn't break.

I slid down to the floor. Every part of me felt numb, yet the pain was still vivid. I sat there, trying to breathe, but every breath moved muscles too close to my stomach. My vision tunneled again, this time so much that I wondered if I'd passed out briefly.

I grabbed the cube again and smashed it against the floor. It shattered on the third try, and I scooped the slime. I didn't even try to examine it before I slapped it against my wound. It sat there for a moment and then absorbed into the bullet hole until it had completely disappeared. I waited for the bleeding to stop, or at least slow. It didn't.

I guess the alien first aid slime didn't work on humans.

I tried to get up, but all I managed was a lazy kick of one foot. My entire body was pretty much numb now. A coldness seeped through me, which was almost soothing. It blanketed the hurt in my gut. My vision tunneled to pure blackness, and I let myself fade into death.

GUESS WHAT? I didn't die.

I knew that because I woke up in a lot of misery. What new hell had I entered? I thought I knew what the world's worst case of flu felt like. I was sorely mistaken. I'd leveled up to the *galaxy's* worst case of the flu by leaps and bounds. My entire body was frigid and shivery, my head pounded, and every hair on my head hurt. I think every nerve ending in my body had been stripped raw. My stomach cramped, and my brain felt like it was soaking in scummy water.

I vaguely recalled my first rule of space travel: I'm not Superman. I sure wish I was. Things would be a lot easier.

I couldn't have been out long because I was still bleeding, and I figured a person had to run out of blood at some point. I dragged myself from the first-aid closet and back into the passageway. As I crawled, shivers wracked me and dizziness nearly toppled me, but somehow, I kept crawling. Mind you, I did this with only one arm *and* a gut wound. The walls had weird alien symbols next to switches, buttons, screens, and metal doors.

One symbol in particular drew my attention. It was a black squiggly circle on a small door halfway up the wall across from me. The symbol seemed thicker than the others.

It also seemed familiar. In my migraine-addled brain, I could almost read the fuzzy symbol as "medical kit." Obviously, I was losing my mind, but since I was dying, I wasn't particularly worried about that. I tried to pull myself up, but all that did was remind me that my legs weren't exactly working, and I found myself on my back with my gut still bleeding. I tried again, knowing I was using up the last ounce of strength in me. Somehow, I propped myself up the wall. I leaned there, eyes closed, for a moment, until I felt like I wasn't going to fall. Then I opened the door.

Inside was a full medical kit. There were needleless syringes, powders, liquids, and—more importantly—bandages. I knew because the three symbols on the package made me think of bandages, and so I went with my gut (no pun intended) and tore open the package. Inside was a thin white bandage. I pressed it against my stomach. It melted against my skin, tickling as the clotting bits stopped the bleeding. Alien band-aids clearly had some excellent blood clotting features.

I grabbed one syringe. The symbols translated "emergency bioformic repair." I went with the hallucination, injected it into my stomach near the wound. Then I dropped the syringe and slumped to the floor.

And that's when I passed out again.

———

This time, I woke up convulsing. There was blood in my mouth from biting my tongue.

I passed out a second later.

———

After several rounds of coming to, only to pass out again, I finally reclaimed consciousness for longer than a few seconds. I lay on my back in the Dyson sphere's passageway, feeling like roadkill. Whatever was in the syringe had helped somewhat because I was no longer suffering from the flu from hell. I'd downgraded to a migraine from hell, a stomach that felt like I'd just birthed a rhino, and a body that felt like a corpse.

Maybe I was a zombie. Maybe the slime or the syringe had turned me into the living dead, or undead, or whatever you call them. My brain was really struggling, so I wasn't trying too hard to get things right. I wondered if something I'd taken had made me feel crappier, or if it was all from the gunshot wound. Being a nineteen-year-old-guy from Nebraska, I didn't exactly have a lot of experience with being shot.

I glanced around me at all the symbols. It was really odd that I could still understand them, or at least my hallucinating brainpan was telling me I could understand them. I went to push up my glasses and then I realized they weren't on my face anymore. I felt around for them and only found the spent syringe. Then, I remembered I'd left them back near the airlock.

But the passageway wasn't fuzzy. All the symbols were clear. I could see okay without my glasses. I held up the syringe. That crap really worked. Curious, I peeled back a corner of the bandage, which turned out to be a big mistake. The bandage was helping a scab form, but it was all stuck together, and I pulled some of the fresh skin off with it. Weirdly, the bullet had fallen out and was not stuck in the bandage.

There was no exit wound, and I'd been more than a bit worried about a chunk of metal somewhere in my guts. But whatever was in the syringe must've been the closest thing to magic that I'd ever seen. I plucked the bullet free. It was a small ball bearing that looked like it was made of plastic. Not what I expected. I tossed it away and pressed the bandage back over my skin. I left the bandage alone after that.

I kept my fingers crossed that the first aid treatment would also prevent an infection. But, even if I didn't get an infection, I had no *freaking ship*.

I tried to reach Fetch via my tablet, but there was no response. I needed to get to my helmet to attempt to reach Fetch that way. I tried to stand but didn't have any strength in me. I lay back down and stared up at the ceiling that seemed to be just a long soft light. If I didn't die from my wound, I'd die from dehydration or hunger. Maybe not dehydration. There'd definitely been water in here for the squid, so I just had to find that. As for hunger, ugh. I hated going hungry. I was one of those guys who could eat an entire pizza and still be hungry. God, I missed pizza. I stared up at the light, fantasizing about pizza, until I finally fell asleep.

I slept on and off for over a day before I could finally crawl over to my helmet and check the HUD. I pocketed my broken glasses even though it didn't seem like I needed them anymore. But if the magic syringe was temporary, I'd need my glasses again—even if both lenses were cracked.

I sat on the floor near the airlock with my helmet on, trying to reach Fetch, but she never responded. At least I knew she was still nearby—after giving up trying to reach her, I struggled to my feet and peered out at her through the airlock window. Outside, a CME shot in the distance, and I'd come to watch them like they were shooting stars. They were pretty as long as they weren't too close.

As for *Fetch*, our attacker had left her adrift as if she were some kind of derelict, no different from the heavily damaged Archivist ship I'd been clearing. With all the rounds she'd taken, to be honest, she probably was... which meant I was stuck in the sphere forever. Injured, weak, light-headed, starving, and parched.

I returned to the first aid kit and hit myself up with another dose of the bioformic repair since it the first dose had helped immensely. My bleeding had stopped, and the sharp pain had dulled to a cramping ache. I was still injured, weak, light-headed, dizzy, starving, and parched, but after a few minutes, I could walk a bit more steadily on my feet.

My first order of business was to find water, which I found in a room a few feet beyond where I'd found the medical kit. The room seemed to be a small lounge, and it had a "sustenance dispenser." At least that's how the symbols translated in my mind. I didn't know how I could read it, but I was definitely reading the weird language and not hallucinating. I had to rummage through a cabinet to find a bowl (there were no cups). When I stood before the dispenser, it scanned me, and a menu appeared, listing what I assumed were acceptable options for my biology.

First up, I ordered water. That seemed like a universally safe choice, but I smelled the liquid before I drank it. I drank three bowls before filling a fourth and taking a seat on a flat cushioned ottoman I assumed had been a chair to whomever had lived here.

The water helped a lot. Within a few minutes, my pounding migraine lessened to a pounding headache. My stomach growled and gurgled, and I had a feeling I'd need a bathroom pretty soon. Knowing my Tardigrades, I was surprised I hadn't needed a bathroom twenty hours ago. I could actually feel the Tardigrades inside me, which was a first. It was a weird sensation of little pricks under my skin and throughout my body. It didn't hurt or tickle, but it was noticeable, and I wondered if they were being extra active because of the extra radiation that bombarded me before I reached the sphere. Or maybe there was some toxin in the sphere itself they were fighting. But, as long as it had air, pressure, and heat until I recovered enough to get back to *Fetch*, I didn't care.

As I downed the fourth bowl, I grabbed a fresh bowl and asked for food. Something that looked like dead, rotting maggots shot into my bowl. I took a sniff and gagged. It smelled even worse than like dead, rotting maggots. I was starving, but I wasn't *that* starving to try maggot casserole... yet. I set the bowl down and decided it was time to take a tour.

With all the damage to the sphere, I was limited to a single passageway of roughly a half-mile long, with blast doors sealing both ends. The Archivists had likely selected this section since it was still functioning. The screens at each end said the passageways on the other sides were compromised and too damaged to enter. I could spend a month investigating this area, which was a miniscule fraction of one percent of the entire sphere that enveloped a star.

I figured the heat inside the passageway came from the star and that there must've been a system running to keep the air from boiling me. Whoever built this place had been way ahead of Earth in terms of technology. That the systems still ran after thousands, if not millions, of years with no maintenance was pretty impressive.

The water helped with the weakness and lightheadedness, though I definitely needed food and probably a blood bag or five. I'd worked up an appetite while clearing the Archivist ship before the mysterious attacker showed up. That was over a day ago. I was famished now.

I kept drinking water, which helped some, but I was still shaky and felt like a spaceship had plowed through me. My stomach hurt and I couldn't even hold my hand against it since I needed it to hold on to a wall. I was miserable and alone in the middle of a system no one ever went to for a very good reason.

I wanted to kill whoever it was that wanted to kill me. I assumed they were those bounty hunters-slash-assassins who'd gone after me in Lohoa Station, but why would they bother to shoot up *Fetch* when they could've just gone straight for me? Probably because they were dicks. So far, every Calcar I'd met was a dick. Then again, that was a fitting description of every alien I'd ever met. People used to annoy me when I was on Earth. After all, my best friend took the girl who took my virginity. But dang it, I wished I was back on Earth now. I'd hug and kiss every human I came across, even my ex-girlfriend. But not my ex-best friend. I have to draw the line somewhere.

Hugs and kisses would come after eating the world's biggest steak and then the cheesiest, sauciest Canadian bacon pizza. My stomach growled, and it hurt—that's how tender my gut still was. I glanced at the bowl of dead maggots sitting on the counter. If I squinted, it almost looked like a bowl of rice with flecks of chives.

I picked up the bowl and smelled it. Shouldn't have done that. I tried not to sniff as I pinched some food between my fingers and shoved it in my mouth.

And then I set a Guinness World Record for going from feeling okay to throwing up in a nanosecond. I hadn't even swallowed. It was the flavor that had done it. Sour, curdled milk mixed with raw frog's legs—that was the image that came to mind. While the water in this food machine didn't have an expiration date, the food inside it clearly did... and had obviously expired several centuries earlier.

When my stomach growled, it hurt. When I threw up, it was the purest, worst agony I'd ever felt in my life. I cried and even sobbed after my stomach quit heaving, and I may have even prayed for death at some point in there. I lay there quaking and shivering (and crying) until the pain ebbed. It felt like forever, but eventually, I could get to my feet and begin the process of drinking water all over again.

I'd only thrown up water and bile, so at least the mess wasn't horrible, but it still smelled, which wasn't great since I had to step over it to get to my water supply. It took another forever before I quit shivering, and I went back to figuring out if there was a machine around here that dispensed miracles.

I decided I'd check out each room in more detail. Most rooms had computer screens, and all looked to serve a different purpose, so I started with the room next door, which turned out to be an engineering interface unit. It was cool that I could read squiggly language and wondered if I'd be able to read other languages, too, now. Even understanding the language, I didn't understand the Engineering codes. It was all sorts of math and numbers. I could see there were problems with most of the systems, which reminded me of Fetch. Worse, if I was reading the warning messages correctly, the Dyson Sphere was on the brink of collapse and about to turn the star into a black hole. No wonder the star had been spitting out CMEs left and right. It was about to blow. Even though I could read the language, I didn't understand the time indicator—it was too different from what I'd grown up with or the intergalactic standard. For all I knew, things could go kaboom in another hour or another millennium. But since the message was flashing red, I had a feeling it was closer to the former than the latter. There was no Easy button to reset the star or the sphere, so I decided to move on and avoid that room.

Next up was the resources room, which I assumed was the equivalent of a human resources room, but the system was down. Same problem with the supplies room. Guess I wouldn't be able to requisition a spaceship patch kit any time soon. But it was full of what looked like game consoles. I made a mental note to load those up with me to sell.

The room after that was the Navigation room, which contained maps of the galaxy, maybe even more galaxies. On each of the maps were dozens of warpgates and warpflows. I had no idea there were so many. Since none of this would help me, I didn't waste time. Before I left there, I found a golden cube in one cabinet, buried under a pile of wiring. Unlike the large, solid data cube I'd found on the Archivist ship, this one fit in the palm of my hand. This cube had a hollowed center, which made me think it wasn't a data cube like the one I'd taken from the Neptar. This small cube enclosed a square circuit board and inside that was a small window of black, but when I peered closer, I could see what looked like a star system. I thought it looked cool, so I pocketed it to sell at the Undermarket.

The race that had built, or at least worked in this sphere, seemed obsessed with squares and cubes. Nearly all the computer screens were square, even the doorways were square-shaped. I wondered why they were so into cubes, but I didn't feel like burning much energy thinking about something I'd never get the answer to.

I enjoyed the records room the most. Using the screen, I could see schematics on the sphere, how it was made up of millions of little sections like the one I was currently in. The way I saw it, the Dyson sphere was a giant Lego ball. The star-facing side of the sphere was made up of some special material that helped convert the energy coming out from the star into power that was used for the sphere along with thousands of space docks.

The history was fascinating. The architecture of this particular Dyson sphere had been the eighty-seventh iteration of its creators. Its eighty-six predecessors had failed and caused their stars to become black holes and destroyed hundreds of star systems. Talk about taking the iterative design process to the extreme.

Fetch would've loved this data, and I wished there was a way to get it to her. I scrolled through the menu hoping to find an export feature and was surprised to find one. It displayed an image of a cube exactly like the one I'd taken from the Archivist ship and noted that the cube it needed to load data into was missing. I guess Fetch could read all that data after all. My brief moment of optimism faded. If Fetch was still alive, she would've come for me, or at least tried to communicate with me.

All the rooms were interesting, but none of them provided me with the miracle I needed. I left the records room to drink more water. Once I was relatively confident the bandage had sealed my wound, I'd pulled my suit back on, sans helmet, to stay warm. Another benefit of wearing the suit was it had a built-in bathroom, though I'd have to find an ejection port around here somewhere. Essentially, I was a walking RV. Just hook me up to water and power, then pump me out every now and then.

As my pain subsided, I noticed I was standing a straighter, which meant I bumped my head on the ceiling. Whoever designed this place couldn't have been taller than four feet since the ceilings were barely four feet high, and I wondered if they were some distant relatives of Oompa Loompas.

As I passed the small room where I'd slathered myself with goo, I paused at the red cross on the door. I'd assumed it was a medical symbol, but now that I could understand this weird alien language, I realized it wasn't a medical symbol at all.

It was a warning that translated to "keep out."

No wonder I had to press so many buttons to get to the slime. I wasn't supposed to get to the slime. I glanced down at my stomach and gingerly ran my hand over it. What alien slime did I slather all over my open wound? Did I just give myself something like Calcarian herpes? Worse?

Of all the rooms, this one didn't have a computer screen, and I realized that was because it was just a storage room—a prison cell for whatever deadly alien virus I'd released.

If I didn't die from my gunshot wound or starvation, this virus would be the end of me.

I slumped down to the floor.

"Crap."

5 /   PATCHES AND
      PRAYERS

I stood inside the airlock, with my helmet in place and suit fully sealed, staring out at *Fetch* in the distance.

If I was going to have any chance of survival, I had to get out of this sphere and back to Fetch's medical system. That meant I had to get to my ship. My hab-suit has thrusters on it, but the thing is, I was terrified of using them. I'd have to use tiny little jets that burned through my suit's power to travel a whole lot farther through space than suits were made to travel. It's a weird feeling, like being scared of heights, but worse because the heights would be all around me. There's no ground in space, and that's terrifying.

I reached up to press the button, and a surge of lightheadedness nearly toppled me. I shook my head to clear it. I would've taken a few deep, calming breaths and meditated the shit out of my fear, but my gut was still too sore, so instead, I muttered what every good action hero muttered, "Screw it," and tapped the button.

The outer door opened, and my feet stayed

planted on the floor. Fear had stiffened my legs, and my breaths were short and loud in my helmet with maybe a little whimpering thrown in. I had to grab the doorframe and pull myself out. As soon as I was free, I wanted to spin and grab a handhold, but Fetch was sitting a fair distance from the sphere and just as far from the Archivist ship, so if I held onto the line to the Archivist ship or walked along the sphere's exterior, I'd just be wasting my time.

I pumped a quick burst on my suit's thrusters and flew forward. It wasn't an aggressive movement, but I twisted painfully as I moved forward. Fetch had told me to always do quick pumps or else I'd burn through my suit's power, so I tried to do that. The power thrusters were tiny jets on my back, integrated with the suit, and the two power buttons were in front of my hips, kind of where a holster would go. Each button could be depressed in the center or at any edge for maneuvering. Since I only had one arm, I had to reach over and tap the left thruster to keep me from veering off. In a way, it was like rowing, where I had to keep switching sides to go straight, and the repetition helped me get into a rhythm that I could focus on rather than obsess over my fear.

I slowly closed the distance as the radiation timer on my HUD slowly counted down. *Fetch* was dark and I could see punctures throughout her hull. At least no holes looked too big to be patched, which meant that hopefully I could patch them and that was all she needed. I also noticed the cargo bay door stood open, and I scowled. The bastards had robbed me.

As my ship loomed larger, I had to maneuver more because I realized I was overshooting her. The distance closed too quickly, and whatever I did just seemed to make me go faster, and I shot wide.

"Crap!"

My fear returned full force then, which caused my lightheadedness to return, and my vision tunneled. I tamped down my nerves while I struggled to change my trajectory and line up for a second approach. This time, I lined up on the center of the ship. I was still way too fast, but instead of shooting wide, I smashed against the hull. I now know what it's like when a bug hits a windshield. At least I fared better than a bug... barely. I'd held my arm over my chest to take the brunt, but the impact was still enough to make my wound send a whimper straight up my windpipe and out of my mouth.

I nearly tumbled over and off my ship, but somehow managed to grab a handhold in time. My shoulder was nearly yanked out of its socket, but I didn't let go, which meant that I slammed against the ship a second time by holding on rather than sliding off. My gut nearly got its vengeance by making me throw up, but I swallowed back the bile in time. I wondered if I threw up in my helmet, while in zero-G, if I'd drown in my own vomit. It wasn't a pleasant thought.

As soon as I could breathe through the pain, I clicked on my mag-boots and walked swiftly over the hull and into the cargo bay. The first thing I noticed was the missing courier drone. The second thing I noticed was most of the cabinets stood open. Some contents were missing, like my cool X-stream deck-rider. That broke a bit of my heart. At least most of my things were crappy enough that they weren't worth stealing. What remained floated loosely, connected to its assigned storage unit by restraining straps, a standard procedure on anything in a cargo bay that was often without gravity. I hustled through the cargo bay and into the main portion of the ship, which I found in the same condition. Cabinets opened, contents missing or strewn loosely about. Tsara's goons had been thorough looting in my ship.

I hustled to the cockpit. Everything was dark. I got down on one knee and flipped the switch under the control panel. Fetch had told me about that after the time we went through a black matter clump.

A single screen displayed a blinking red cursor before a message slowly typed out.

SYSTEMS UNABLE TO LOAD. THE FOLLOWING TWO CRITICAL FAILURES MUST BE RESOLVED PRIOR TO REBOOT:

1. MULTIPLE HULL BREACHES CAUSING RADIATION AND TEMPERATURE CONCERNS

2. POWER SYSTEMS FAILURE, ALL BACKUP BATTERIES DRAINED

REBOOT UPON RESOLVING CRITICAL FAILURES

The patching needed to happen first. Ship hulls are essentially hab-suits for ships. With breaches, ships can get damaged by radiation, too. Sure, they can handle a lot more than someone like me, but radiation will still eat away at the wiring and systems as badly as acid.

I hustled down the passageway, pausing at the food station. I tested it, but it didn't power on. I remembered my dad's obsession with extra food —I realized he was practical rather than obsessed —and I opened a drawer next to the food station. Meal bars floated out from the drawer, and I grabbed each one and pocketed it. At least the Calcars avoided the food area. I made a mental note that the food area was probably a great place to hide valuables from looters, since every race ate different foods.

With my pockets bulging with frozen bars, I went to level two to grab the hull patch kit. Which the thieves had stolen. I thumped my helmet against the cabinet door, thinking of a Plan B. When it hit me, I strode to the cargo bay and grabbed a small laser torch—it'd been too small and too old for the thieves to be interested in it, but if I didn't find my bazooka, then this could be a lifesaver. With the radiation timer in my HUD constantly counting down, I couldn't waste time. I stood at the open cargo bay door, released my mag-boots, and jumped off.

CMEs shot out in the distance like a meteor shower. I didn't know how close one would have to be to vaporize me, and I didn't want to find out.

By the time I reached the Archivist ship, I was getting a pretty good feel for spacewalking, but my suit needed a longer break in between spacewalks because I was draining its power faster than it could recharge. I was feeling the same way. Without food and rest, I was feeling weaker by the minute. I landed on the ship with less pain this time and entered. I'd hoped to grab their patch kit, but the thieves hadn't forgotten about this ship. I spent a few minutes searching for the patch kit, anyway, with no luck.

Onto Plan C. I walked the outside of the wreck, searching for hunks of hull that were nearly torn off.

On a positive note, I found my bazooka torch. It had snagged on the torn hull, and the thieves had missed it. On a negative note, my missing arm was nowhere to be found. Seriously, who the hell steals prosthetic arms? Evidently, asshole Calcars.

Having my left arm would've made things a lot easier. Instead, I had to cut holding the torch in my right hand while using my legs and back to help hold me in position. The muscle strain did not please my gut. I quickly discovered a problem with Plan C. It took *forever* to cut an inch. It would take months to cut enough patches at this rate.

Onto Plan D. Except I didn't have a Plan D.

My radiation alert sounded, and I hurried back to the sphere. I held the restraining cable, but I'd become comfortable enough spacewalking that I held on more out of a sense of security than anything.

Once inside, I took off my helmet and went straight for a meal bar. These bars didn't use plastic wrappers that you see on Earth, otherwise space would be full of wrappers, straws, and water bottles. Instead, they had a waxy coating that was edible. I tried to take a bite and nearly broke a tooth.

I placed the frozen bar against my cheek to thaw it, which was a stupid mistake. I hadn't noticed how cold it was since I was still wearing my hab-suit glove. The bar wasn't just freezer-frozen; it was colder than Satan's nipples. I dropped the bar, hissing in pain, thankful it hadn't stuck to my skin. As I cupped my cheek, I stared longingly at the food. When the pain went down somewhat, I picked up the bar and went to the small lounge.

I grabbed a bowl. As it filled with water, I set out meal bars along the counter to thaw. My mouth watered. I'd tried one of those bars before—they tasted chalky and were so chewy they'd stick to my teeth for a day. But lined up on the counter, they looked like the most delicious thing in the universe.

I set one bar in water, hoping being soaked would make it thaw faster. I even blew on it as if that could help. I peeled off my glove using my teeth and kept checking the bar, trying to bend it. As soon as it bent in the slightest, I took it out and carefully took a bite. I had to bite hard and chew even harder, but the first taste of nourishment was pure ecstasy.

One bar was supposed to be a day's worth of food. I ate two bars and then drank the now-greenish water I'd used to soak the bars.

Already, I could feel my energy returning.

I felt like I could eat more, but I had a feeling I was going to feel overstuffed the way it was, so I returned to the project of fixing my ship. I pulled out my tablet and went to the supplies room first and scanned one of the Xboxes. My tablet was simply an interface with Fetch, but it had some minimal search capabilities on its own. The tablet came back with *Unknown*, but it listed likely candidates, the first of which were power boosters. I grabbed three, one at a time, and placed them by the airlock.

I had to take a break after that. My stomach was cramping too much, and I felt like I was about to go into a food coma, so I returned to the lounge. I tried to curl up in that weird chair, but my gut wasn't having that, so I lay on my back on the floor. It didn't take me long to fall asleep.

———

I woke up with a Plan D. Well, it was really Plan C at a different location. With my suit reporting normal radiation, I reset the timer and headed back outside. This time, I walked across the sphere until I came to the next section over. This section had a big gash through its hull. I tried out the bazooka on the material, and lo and behold, it cut through like butter. I was more than a little surprised because I expected it to not to even make a dent being made by some super advanced civilization.

I cut off as big of a piece as I could carry and flew out to *Fetch*. I lined it up over an area that had been perforated with over a dozen holes to see how it'd fit. When it touched the hull, it kind of just melted against it, filling the holes.

"Whoa." I stared.

I'd been just seeing how much it'd cover. I'd had no idea how I was going to actually adhere the stuff with a patch kit. Evidently, it was self-healing. It might not be strong enough to fly a warpflow, but as long as it's strong enough to get the hell out of Dodge, I was happy.

I returned to the sphere and began the cycle

of cutting off material and sticking it onto my ship. On the fourteenth trip to *Fetch* and five radiation breaks later, I tried to fill a hole that was larger than the others, and I discovered the material could only self-heal smaller holes. For that spot, I stuffed some broken-off hull into the breach to until I formed a clunky web, and the webbing sealed together.

Fortunately, the remaining patching went easy. After I scoured the hull for any remaining breaches and being pleased with my handiwork, I smiled. "Now I call that a *hullistic* approach to patching a ship."

Since Fetch was still offline, there was no one to tell me how bad my jokes were (I already knew they were bad). Still, I decided to save that line for my memoir. Fetch would enjoy reading it then.

After another radiation break, I returned to my ship with the three battery packs in tow. With only one arm, I had to loop them together with a rope which I'd tied around my waist. I flew slower, not wanting to damage them when I banged into my ship, which I had a knack of doing every single time. If you think momentum on Earth is bad, you should see what it's like in space.

I reached my ship and hustled as quickly as I could into the still-open cargo bay since the door wouldn't close without power. I wanted to kiss whoever came up with mag-boots—they made getting around in zero-G so much easier.

I'd grabbed three Xboxes since I knew the ship had three backup battery slots. In space, ships didn't just have redundancies; they had redundancies for their redundancies. I untied and strapped the first Xbox onto the charger shelf above the battery. There were no charging cables, which were typical of the more advanced batteries. I was hoping these Xboxes were similar enough in technology to work. I mean, a battery's a battery, right?

Nothing happened for several seconds before the screen lit up on the ship's backup battery, and it showed its charging rate. It climbed from zero percent to three percent in only a few seconds. Relief flooded me, and I even did a little happy dance. I hadn't really expected my guess to work. I hustled to the two other backup batteries. Both were located in the front half of the ship, with one on level 2 (top level) and the other on level 3 (bottom level).

I sure was glad that Fetch had shown me all the important bits of the ship and covered all the emergency procedures during our long trips. Otherwise, I never would've known where to start. She'd talk through various procedures as I worked on fixes around the ship. She'd said that it was required of ship computers to train their crew, but I think she would've trained me, anyway, although *training* is a far cry from *doing*. The next time (hopefully there'd never be a next time) that I'd have to patch the hull or spacewalk, I'd certainly be more efficient.

I strode to the cockpit on level 1 and flipped the system switch again. I figured at least one battery had charged by the time I'd finished placing the other two chargers. The screen loaded and red dots ran down the screen as the system did whatever systems had to do.

SYSTEMS LOADING…

As soon as I saw the message, I felt the first surge of hope since the attack. I would've plopped into my chair except plopping doesn't work in zero-G. So instead I stood smugly, waiting to hear Fetch's voice in my helmet.

And waited.

Fetch's husky voice never came through. Eventually, more text displayed on a single screen.

Hello, Frank. I'm back online but operating at minimum operational capacity. I require more power to start all environmental systems.

Well, crap.

"I can get you more battery packs," I said.

If the ship had full pressure and atmosphere, uninterruptible power backup supplies would maintain minimally required levels. However, I require additional power to bring up the environmental, propulsion, and navigation systems to sustainable levels.

Well, double crap.

"I don't know what to do."

There was a lengthy delay before she "spoke" again. *My databanks show that the Dyson sphere contains innumerable space docks. I had previously located one that still shows power readings. Once all backup batteries are fully recharged, I will use all three—rather than pulling from only one at a time—to propel to the dock and recharge there.*

"Okay. How long's that going to take?"

The batteries are nearly charged. But propulsion will be minimal. I do not have enough power to run engines; therefore, I'll need to use direc-

tional thrusters. It will take seven hours for me to dock. Until I connect to the dock, I cannot estimate how many hours it will take to recharge.

That was a long time. "Uh, what do you want me to do?"

Since you cannot remain onboard for the duration, given current radiation levels, I need your authorization to self-propel to the dock.

"You've got it, of course."

Excellent. I'm powering up directional thrusters. I advise you to reenter the sphere for radiation protection.

"You knew I was there?"

I calculated that an intact portion of the sphere could be the only possible place for your survival, my delicate Terran.

It was the first hint of Fetch's charm returning, which made me feel like we had a chance more than ever.

"All right. I'll be watching you from the sphere."

I will notify you when I've recharged enough that we can begin repairs.

I tapped the instrument panel—it was the closest thing to squeezing her shoulder—and left my ship. Dozens of small directional thrusters were glowing around the hull, though it looked like she'd powered up less than a third of them.

I hated leaving her behind, but there was nothing I could do. I returned to the sphere and waited.

———

Fetch took four freaking days to recharge enough to bring all systems to minimal functionality. During that time, I had to pull an environmental management box (among a gazillion other parts) from the Archivist ship to replace ours that was beyond repair. I also transferred a lot more exterior 'skin' from the sphere and more or less wrapped my ship, per Fetch's instructions. Evidently, I'd skimped too much on the original patching. I also think she liked the feel of the new material on her hull, especially since it kind of melted around ports, cameras, and sticky-outy things like handles, thrusters, and engines.

When I was finished with the outside, I had to do the same on the inside, patching the many, *many* bullet holes (I quit counting at seventy-six).

Even with all that work, it took another two days before the interior was purged of radiation enough that I could work inside without wearing my spacesuit. During that time, I kept busy working on emergency repairs. If I dozed off, she'd wake me up by blaring an alarm.

Fetch is not a lot of fun when she's broken. She's even less fun when docked at a Dyson sphere enclosing a star about to go supernova. We were bugs sitting on top of the galaxy's largest, ticking atomic bomb.

That motivated both of us to work as fast as we could, as hard as we could. Fetch's mini drones worked mostly on fixing cabling and piping that I couldn't easily reach. Plus, they were a lot more surgical than I could be. As Fetch put it, I treated every tool in my toolbox, including my head, like a hammer. I disagreed, but it's hard to argue with a computer who can play videos proving my guilt.

I finished packing insulation around an open wiring compartment in the cargo bay, and then stood stiffly and stretched, careful not to over-stretch my sore stomach muscles. "I feel like I'm eighty. Is that a symptom of radiation poisoning?"

"No. It's a symptom of not being in great shape."

"Be nice. I was shot only a week ago."

"And my sensors read that you are nearly fully healed. You clearly found excellent first aid supplies either in the Archivist vessel or in the sphere. You should bring any remaining supplies with us. They seem to have worked exceptionally well, though I've noticed you are eating far more than normal."

"I'd grab more if I could, but I used all the magic syringes," I said.

"Ideally, you won't get shot again, but as you've been shot twice and haven't been a recla-mation agent for even a year, I think the more emergency supplies we have, the better. As for the treatment you used; since it clearly wasn't designed for Terran anatomy, we should monitor you for long-term symptoms."

"I think that's a really good idea," I said, shiv-ering at the idea of the slime.

"What did you do, Frank?"

"I didn't do anything. Why do you ask?"

"Your voice wavered, and you have that look like you broke something, and you don't want to tell me."

"I didn't break anything, I swear."

"Knowing you, I imagine I'll find out soon

enough. So, are you ready for the next task?" she asked.

I scowled. "Gimme ten minutes. I'm going on like two hours of sleep, tops."

"You've slept three hours and twelve minutes over the past twenty-four hours. That is adequate for a man your age during extraordinary circumstances."

"You know, I wish I'd shot that Calcar, Tsara. Then she wouldn't be alive to send assassins after me and shoot us both up."

"It wasn't the pair of assassins who gave chase at Lohoa Station," Fetch said.

I jerked. "Then who the heck were they?"

"It was a lone CCC agent."

"The who what?" I asked.

"Cosmic Claims Consultants are Triple-S's biggest competitor. They are unscrupulous and the second highest cause of death for new reclamation agents, second only to being killed while reclaiming items from those who do not wish to have their items taken."

"And I'm just finding out about these guys now?"

"There was no reason to concern you with information that would cause you unnecessary anxiety."

"There's reason, trust me. If I'd known Triple-S had some serious cutthroat competition out there, I would've done something about it."

"Like what?"

I thought, and then shrugged. "I dunno. *Something.*" I frowned. "So that's why the courier drone was stolen. I assumed they just took it while they pillaged my ship."

"No, it was a lone Calcar who goes by the name of Krallix. He pillaged your ship after he took the drone. Your father had several run-ins with him. Your father referred to him as 'murderous scum.'"

"Sounds about right," I said. "This murderous scum who stole the drone has probably already got the bounty from it."

"No. Calcars are notoriously suspicious. They don't use courier drones, and they would never trust their employer to send them payment. They always deliver in person so they can get paid in person. We have three months to catch up with Krallix, assuming he's delivering the drone to the nearest CCC office."

"Good," I said. "That gives us time to catch up to him."

"I strongly advise against giving chase to a Calcar with a railgun. I recommend we contact Totty; she will understand."

"She won't," I said.

"You're right; she won't. But she also *likely* won't kill you, while Krallix certainly will, with glee."

I considered her words. "We have a problem. Krallix took the artifact that was sitting on top of the drone, right?" I asked.

"He did."

"That artifact's a memory stick from the sphere. It even details how to create your own Dyson sphere."

"How do you know that?"

"I read about it when I was hanging around, trying not to die, in the sphere."

"The sphere's interface includes English?"

"No. The first aid shot also gave me a universal translator," I said.

"Emergency treatments don't include language interfaces or brain manipulation. What did you do, Frank?"

"Again with the accusations."

"If what you say is true, that data needs to be destroyed or turned over to Jack. Dyson spheres are highly unstable and deemed illegal."

Jack was our handler with the Galactic Oversight Directorate—GOD for short. I'd only met Jack once, and we didn't especially get along. It ticketed me for emissions—a fine that set me back a month.

"Think Jack would pay us to turn in that kind of data?" I asked.

"Possibly. GOD's rationality tends to not always seem rational," she said. "But if we do not reclaim such a data cube and deliver it directly to GOD, then we'd be deemed as guilty as Krallix."

"That means we've got to go after Krallix no matter what to get GOD that data cube. And we gotta get our stuff back. Wait, something just hit me. If Krallix was the one who shot us up, then where are Tsara's goons?"

"Likely very close to reaching us. We have three emergency repairs remaining before I can safely power up the engines. I'll begin plotting a course to intercept Krallix. He cannot enter a warpflow without going offline first to repair his engine. With luck, we'll reach him before his engine repairs are complete."

"He's got a bad engine?"

"I rammed his engine. Poor planning on his

part for having a ship with only a single engine." I could hear the smugness in her voice.

I wiped my hands on my pants. "All right, let's wrap up these repairs and get out of here."

"I'm afraid we have a problem."

"What's that?"

"I'm reading a massive buildup within the sphere. That star is going supernova."

Light through cracks in the Dyson sphere was glowing brighter and brighter, and I gulped. "Um, Fetch, you can get us out of here anytime now."

"I started working on that as soon as I picked up the new readings. I advise you to secure yourself to something. I anticipate the next several minutes to be rather tumultuous, should we survive that long."

"I'd better get my hab-suit on."

"There's no time."

I was thrown to the floor from the ship tumbling from the dock and the artificial gravity inside playing catch up. My stomach gave me a sharp cramp in protest, but adrenaline tamped down any pain, and I ran to the nearest open locker. I grabbed the tie strap that was connected to the wall of the locker to keep gear from being jostled around, stepped inside, and tied it around my chest, just under my armpits, to help hold me in place.

Gravity and lights disappeared in the next

second, and panic gripped me. "Uh, Fetch, I'm not gonna lose my air or heat, am I?"

"My engines need all available power. I will restart critical systems once we clear the supernova."

"We're going to clear the supernova, right?"

"Theoretically, it's possible. Realistically, it's not likely."

With the locker door still standing open, I gaped out of a small round window at the Dyson sphere. After so many years of wearing glasses, out of habit, I went to push up my glasses even though I wasn't wearing them—and maybe (hopefully) I would never need them again.

Outside, the Dyson sphere still loomed before us like a huge Death Star. I chuckled drily when I realized it really was about to become a real-life death star, as in "My Death" Star.

So far, an exploding star was incredibly anti-climactic, though the Dyson sphere seemed to be expanding as it contained whatever the star inside was doing.

What was the opposite of anticlimactic was the way everything around me felt—the ship was shaking apart. Worse, it felt like we weren't even flying yet. It took a long time for ships to build up speed, especially ship's that were limping along.

That's when the star exploded, and shit got real. Light burst out from the seams of the sphere, which must've doubled in size to contain it. The sphere grew faster than we were flying, and it was riding up our tailpipe. There's not much pressure in space, but the sphere was pushing whatever miniscule amount of pressure there was right at us. Believe it or not, the ship smoothed out and I could feel us picking up speed. We still weren't fast enough.

Rays of intense starlight shot out through holes and fractures in the sphere, with one ray shooting by so close that I was blinded for a few moments. I really wished I had my hab-suit on for extra protection, but then I realized that if the sphere hit us at that speed, we'd be squashed against it, leaving only a splat behind.

Seconds before it smashed into us, its expansion slowed and then stopped. All light from within it went dark, and no CMEs shot out.

Once I could find my breath again, I said, "That was a close one."

Then the sphere began to shrink. So slowly at first that I didn't notice, thinking it was just Fetch accelerating from it. But as the sphere shrank faster, the movement was unmistakable. The ship shook, and I wondered if the sphere was trying to pull us back to it, because it sure felt that way.

Soon, the sphere was shrinking as quickly as it'd expanded, like a rubber band that had been stretched. My ship vibrated more and more, the faster the sphere shrank. The sphere shrank until it seemed smaller than it had been before. Soon, it was definitely smaller than it was before.

"Uh, Fetch, something's happening out there."

"You don't want to know," Fetch said. "I'm running at maximum available power, but it may not be enough."

"Enough for what?" I asked.

"Enough to escape the pull of the black hole," she replied.

"Black hole? What black hole? Oh, crap."

Then I saw what she was talking about. The supernova didn't just explode; it also imploded, and it sucked the Dyson sphere into it. The sphere could only shrink so much, and when it reached that threshold, it crumpled like a tin can. It disappeared in a sarlaac pit of darkness. Glints of starlight and debris swirled around the outer edge, which I assumed to be the event horizon. The whirlpool reminded me of a mega-sized toilet flushing. The hole's maw was growing bigger every second.

"Uh, Fetch, how're we doing?" I asked.

"I don't like our odds," she replied.

I flinched, but then remembered that Fetch was an eternal pessimist. "But would I like the odds?"

"I doubt it."

"Well... are you going to tell me the odds?"

"I can't. The black hole is growing at an inconsistent rate. The odds change every time I run a calculation."

"Are they better than fifty percent, at least?" I asked.

"Only if I use the most favorable assumptions."

"I'll take it."

I continued to stare out the window, watching as the black hole grew and its event horizon spread out farther and farther. The ship rattled and shook, and I wondered how much of that was from fighting the black hole's pull or if the ship was just in that bad of shape. As the hole grew, the ship rattled more, which answered my question. We were trying to escape a freaking black hole.

My stomach cramped, but I ignored it. I was too focused on the ship's frame where a bolt had just gone flying off.

I opened my mouth to ask Fetch about it, but clamped it shut. I didn't think I'd like the answer.

Believe it or not, I fell asleep. Or I might've blacked out. After several hours of fleeing a black hole with the tenacity of a junkyard dog, I'd ended up with a killer migraine and a cramping stomach. When I woke up some time later, the black hole was still behind us, but the ship rattled and shook less than before. And since I was still alive, the hull must've still been sealed.

"Glad to see you could rejoin me," Fetch said, sounding a little snarky.

"Are we getting away?" I asked.

"Yes, unless we suffer an engine failure, we should break free from this system within the next three hours. At that point, I have full confidence we'll be at a safe distance from the black hole since it has since stabilized. As black holes go, it is a rather small one."

Relief flooded me, and I yawned. "Wake me in three hours."

Three hours and three days later, I was knee deep working through the fix-it list. We were lucky that Krallix wasn't able to remove the printer. I hadn't realized that 3D printers were considered so crucial to a ship that they were integrated into the ship's frame. Otherwise, I'm sure that Calcar would've taken it.

In a rhythm matching my throbbing headache, I pounded out the bent doorframe connecting the cargo bay to the rest of the ship and tested it to ensure the door opened and closed. I wasn't sure how it got bent in the first place. Based on what I'd seen of Calcars so far, they are hard on everything. I dropped the hammer and stretched my aching back before wiping sweat from my brow. It must've been a hundred degrees in there. "Any luck with the life support system yet, Fetch?"

"I'm having to reroute lines. It will take another hour," she replied.

"I'm going to melt by then," I said. Until I lived in space, I would've assumed that ships had to be constantly heating themselves since space is, you know, *cold*. I had no idea that the opposite was actually true: that ships had to be constantly monitoring and purging extra heat. Evidently, the engine and all the systems running generate a lot of heat that builds up. It was a scientific fact that I was learning firsthand.

I was wearing underwear and nothing else. I would've been able to finish these jobs twice as fast if I still had both arms, and I'd finish them some faster if I had my prosthetic arm. I needed to get that courier drone and artifact back, but I was especially looking forward to getting my left arm back from Krallix. I've yet to meet a Calcar I liked. Then again, I've yet to meet an alien I liked.

I noticed a line that had a fissure in it. I knelt. It wasn't dripping water, so I held my hand over it and felt a light breeze of cooler air. An oxygen line, probably. I pulled out the roll of sealing tape and wrapped it around the line.

At least no crucial systems had been shot, but the ship was in a bad way. I mean, it was in a bad way before. Now, it was in a worse way. I stood to check the fix-it list in the cockpit when a wave of dizziness nearly dropped me.

"You should allow me to run a medical scan. Your blood pressure is too low, and your temperature is elevated," Fetch said.

"Later. Once we get through the priority 1 repairs."

I started walking, and the next thing I knew, I awoke face-down on the grated floor. I groaned and rolled onto my back.

"Now will you allow me to run a medical scan?" Fetch asked.

"I'm probably just dehydrated," I said, which didn't make sense even as I said it. I'd drunk a lake's worth of water back in the sphere.

"We both know that's not the case," she said. Sometimes I wondered if AI computers could read minds.

"If you require medical attention, the sooner I apply care, the faster your recovery. By delaying treatment, you could jeopardize my current legal status," she said.

"Huh?"

"If you die, I'll have to fly back to Totty and who knows who I'll be transferred to. It could be highly inconvenient."

"Oh, well, I'll try not to die since it'd inconvenience you," I said drily.

I climbed to my feet, holding the wall for support just in case, though the dizziness had passed. I made my way to the medical "bay," which consisted of two cabinets in my living quarters. I opened one cabinet and what emerged was a long robotic arm with a variety of contraptions on its Swiss Army "hand." I recognized the probe, laser, and scalpel, but there was plenty more I didn't recognize. The hand rotated through tools until an oblong glass ball was in front. It bore a horizontal red laser line through it.

"Lie still on your bunk. The scan could take several minutes," Fetch said.

"Wake me if I fall asleep," I said.

The scanner started at my feet and moved fast up and down my body. I'd expected it to run glacially slow, but I guess that's just how things worked back home. As it ran, Fetch said, "You've healed much faster than expected from the projectile injury, and you show no signs of infection."

"Do you think the tardigrades would've helped speed up the healing process?" I asked.

"No. Think of them like a specialized kidney. They purge radiation and other impurities that cause damage to bioforms; they aren't healers in the medical sense."

"Oh, then it must've been the first aid kit," I said.

"Perhaps, though surprising, since I've already pointed out that their medicine clearly wasn't formulated for Terran biology."

I bit my lip.

"What aren't you telling me?" she asked.

"Well..." I drawled. "I did try another first aid treatment in the sphere. At least I thought it was first aid at the time. It had the red cross on it."

"The red cross is the universal sign for Do Not Touch—Danger."

"I know that *now*. At the time I didn't know that, and I was in a really bad way. So I opened the compartment and uh, kind of slathered some slime on my wound."

"That was extremely unwise," she said. "You may have exposed yourself to a virus or some other sort of lethal biological agent."

"I know. Like I said, I was a bit desperate and running on fumes right about then. It didn't kill me, so I'm going to be okay, right?"

"I can tell you with high confidence that you are *not* going to be okay. Despite you appearing healthier than ever, there are irregularities in your circulatory system that require a deeper scan. Additionally, my initial scans have come back inconclusive on viral agents, and I'm now running more thorough scans that identify all known biological and technological agents. What I can tell you is that you no longer have any tardigrades in your system. They have been fully purged from your body."

I nearly sat up. "But if I don't have them to fend off the radiation—"

"Yet, your body is fending off radiation better than ever, most likely a carryover from the first aid treatments you self-administered. Now, lie still and quit fidgeting."

I gulped as I lay there awaiting Fetch's diagnosis. "I hope I'm not going to die. I'm too young to die."

"If you didn't slather dangerous chemicals on open wounds, I believe you'd have a much better chance at longer term survival," she said.

"Whatever," I grumbled.

"Well, the deeper scan has been completed. The irregularities in your circulatory system are technoformic in nature."

I sat up. "What?"

"I believe you heard me, so I will not bother to repeat myself. I'm displaying an internal view on the nearest screen now."

I glanced at the cracked screen above my bed (most screens were cracked on the ship—they were cracked before I came onboard). On the screen was a video that reminded me of something I'd seen on some medical show where they were doing surgery, except instead of showing an open cut, this only showed my innards, clear as day. It zoomed in to where the width of a single artery filled much of the screen. Inside it was a long string.

"What the hell is that?" I asked.

"Undetermined. I may need to run an invasive scan."

"Do whatever you have to do. It looks like it's going to give me a heart attack."

"It's too small, and it's already gone through your heart. In fact, it's lengthened through all your arteries and has already begun to weave into your brain. That is likely why you fainted."

"Get it *out* of me," I said.

"It's already integrated enough in your body that removal of it would likely kill you," she said. "However, once I determine exactly what type of technoform this is, I may be able to stop it from spreading further."

"Do whatever you have to do. I don't want to become RoboCop," I said.

"I'm not familiar with that race, but—oh, interesting."

"What's interesting?"

"I have identified that the nonnative species inside you assisted in your recovery. See how it creates nanobots and sends them to your cells to heal you more efficiently? It looks like these tiny organisms are instructing your cells how to heal. Rather fascinating. This would lead me to believe that this is a symbiotic species."

I looked at the screen as the video switched to what looked like bloody muscle, and tendrils were tickling the muscle. It reminded me of a jellyfish except that it was *inside* me. "A symbiote? So is it like Venom then?"

"A symbiont," she corrected. "And I'm not familiar with that race either."

"Venom, as in Spider-Man? You need to read more. Anyway, it doesn't matter. What do we do about it?"

"I cannot give a recommendation without knowing which race of symbiotic technoforms we're dealing with. It must be either quite rare or ancient, as there is nothing in the databases on it. Until I know, I recommend taking a conservative medical approach."

"And that would be?"

"Wait and see."

I scowled. "You're not the one with an alien taking over your body."

"To be precise, the alien inside has not yet attempted to take control of your body. If it did so, that would identify it as an aggressive, predatory species."

"Which we won't know until it tries to take

over my body or kill me, and by then, won't it be too late?" I asked.

"Yes."

"I don't like the wait-and-see approach."

"I'm afraid that is our only option at the moment. I advise you to get dressed. We have caught up with Krallix sooner than anticipated. It seems I damaged *Star Claimer*'s engine more than I thought."

I jumped to my feet and grabbed the bunk to steady myself. I already had a feeling that the jellyfish inside me was going to be a real pain in the butt.

"*Star Claimer* has its engine powered down, but it's safe to assume its scanners are active, and Krallix likely knew we were in his quadrant the same moment we picked up his location. There is no way to sneak onboard and reclaim our stolen goods," she said.

"That's okay, because we're not sneaking in. I've got a plan," I said.

"I never like your plans."

"You're going to like this one even less than usual."

"I expect as much," she said.

"We ram his engine."

"That is not a plan. That's a poorly thought-out action."

I shrugged. "It always works in the movies."

"This is not the movies. Ramming his engine may work, or it may cause an explosion that kills all of us."

I didn't like the sound of that. "What if we ram the side? Breach the hull and kill him."

"For one thing, he would've seen us coming,

so he likely donned a hab-suit already. Ramming him does not have a high likelihood of killing him unless he's at the precise location of impact."

"And the other thing?"

"Ramming another ship also means that we could damage our own ship in the process. The bow is the most fortified part of a ship, but we're not pirates—we don't have an augmented bow."

"But you rammed his engine once already," I said.

"That was out of desperation."

"We're desperate now! Besides, he's a sitting duck. You can hit him at the right speed and angle for minimum damage, right?" I asked.

"Of course."

"Then we'll have to risk it. We don't have any other way out."

"It's a horrible plan."

"Party pooper. Don't tell me you have any better ideas," I said.

"I do, but unfortunately, they all involve items I do not have onboard, many of which were stolen recently. If I may make one suggestion..."

"Shoot," I said.

"That's exactly what Krallix will do once we're within a logistical range. Since his railgun is bow-mounted, I recommend we steer clear of his bow."

"That sounds like a most excellent suggestion."

"I will set a course to ram his stern, the weakest side of his ship. At minimum, we will further damage his engine. If we have any of that luck which you rely so heavily upon, we may breach his hull."

"Breach away," I said and then dressed and donned my hab-suit.

Within ten minutes, I had my blaster holstered on my hip, my bazooka laser cutter on my other hip, and I'd strapped myself in the cargo bay as far from the point of impact as possible. I was ready. I didn't feel ready, but that wouldn't stop me. I've grown up a lot in the last year. Back home, even if I'd hit rock bottom, there still would be options. I was never truly alone. But out here, in space, every day was a fight to survive. If I didn't do whatever was necessary, then I was going to end up dead, plain and simple.

Fetch was relaying the feed from her front cameras through my HUD, so I could watch what was happening outside. We were coming up on *Star Claimer*, the cylindrical ship without a glow in its engine, though lights were on through all the windows. As we approached, it seemed like we were slowing down too much.

"Go faster. We need to breach his hull," I said.

"Faster could breach my hull."

"Can't you find the right balance?"

"This is the right balance. Leave the pilotage to me," she replied.

"I am."

"You are not."

As we closed the distance, I realized we were going faster than I thought, and I tensed up at the inevitable impact. This really was a horrible plan.

Fetch announced, "Impact in three... two... one."

We slammed into *Star Claimer*'s damaged engine. I was glad Fetch had turned off the gravity after I'd strapped in; otherwise, I would've been knocked around. With the residual gravity, I was still jostled.

"How'd we do?" I asked.

"We received only cosmetic damage to our shielding. His engine is beyond repair. The surrounding hull buckled but held," she replied.

"But it always works in the movies," I lamented.

"And I told you, this is no movie."

"Can you reverse and hit him again?"

"I'm not a bumper car. I advise you to move quickly. If *Star Claimer* had gravity, Krallix may be dealing with injuries. I will rotate to align the bay door with his cargo door."

I clumsily unbuckled the tie strap holding me in place and hustled to the cargo bay door, which Fetch was already opening. Funny that I was no longer worried about spacewalking. Then again, I was terrified of going after a Calcar alone, so that terror made anything else feel like a cakewalk.

A bout of dizziness made me curse the alien slime hitching a ride inside me, and then I tried to ignore it. I flew around Fetch and toward the door that I'd seen on the video feed. It was dented from the collision. I reached across and grabbed the laser torch. The moment I reached the door, I started cutting.

Before I accomplished anything beyond a scratch, the door opened, which I hadn't expected. A large Calcar stood in the doorway, grinning. He slapped the torch out of my hand and grabbed me by the neck. I kicked at him, reaching for my blaster, but he punched me in the stomach with his free hand—not good. My stomach had still been sore, and the punch was raw agony. My vision went white.

"Frank, are you alive?"

I coughed and tried to get air.

"If you can hear me, the other Calcarian ship caught up with us, Frank. They're docking onto me now."

I struggled to speak. "Send... distress call," I managed to say right before I completely blacked out.

I CAME AWAKE with a migraine and my wrist tied to a storage rack in a storage room I didn't recognize, which meant I definitely wasn't on my ship. Especially since around me was a lot of my stuff, including the courier drone I needed to ship off to Totty. The cube was sitting on a shelf near me, which gave me some relief. At least I wouldn't have to go searching for it. My helmet was lying in a corner, like Krallix had kicked it away after removing it. I couldn't see the face shield, but I hoped he hadn't broken it. I needed to reach it to talk to Fetch and make sure they didn't shoot her up again. My blaster was next to it, which gave me hope.

But the best thing I saw was my prosthetic arm propped on the same rack I was tied to. I stretched for it, but it was out of my reach, and I sat back down. That's just mean to steal a guy's arm. It hit me then that Krallix was exactly the kind of evil boss I played in video games. I really missed playing video games. Back home, I'd play every chance I could with my stupid best friend who'd been secretly sleeping with my girlfriend.

Clarissa had hated me playing video games—that should've been a red flag. She probably hated them so much because she was an evil boss, too. Anyway, Jacob's probably still playing the games we used to play together, and Clarissa probably still hates them (and hopefully she hates Jacob, too, by now).

I doubted Calcars played video games, which could explain why they were so ill-tempered.

The compartment had a weird smell like old smoked barbeque, but it didn't smell as good as it sounded, more like meat had been rotten before it was cooked, or someone had left it out for way too long afterward. I'd love a good, juicy steak, but this smell didn't make my mouth water in the least. Instead, it gave me a bad feeling in the pit of my gut.

The door to the compartment was closed, but I could hear three gruff Calcar voices arguing in whatever the Calcars called their language. Weirdly, I could understand it now, just like I could read the alien language in the Dyson sphere. Their voices were muffled by the wall, but they spoke loudly and sounded ticked off, though Calcars always sound ticked off. Their language was simple, with only two vowels, and the longest word had a whopping three syllables.

The three were currently arguing about dinner. It sounded like each one was demanding their own roast, but there was only one roast available. Evidently, Calcars refuse to share, and all three felt like they deserved it.

A pot roast did sound pretty good. I blinked slowly when I realized a pot roast sounded horrible because *I* was to be the roast. I remember

Tsara talking about eating me, but I'd assumed she was joking. I now had the feeling that she'd been very serious.

I had to get out of here. Sure, I had to get my stuff, but more importantly, I had to get myself out of here before I became dinner.

I had the galaxy's worst luck.

I tugged at my restraints. It was just a plastic cord, but it was tied too tightly around my wrist to wriggle free. I leaned forward and used my teeth to try to remove my hab-suit glove, but the glove was too long and the cord too tight. I noticed the metal shelving rack was old and beaten up, and the edge looked sharper a few inches higher. I raised my hand. The cord was tied tightly enough that it didn't move easily, but I managed.

As I worked the cord up and down against the sharper edging of the rack, I found slack, and my motions became faster. There wasn't enough room to free my hand, so I worked even faster, given I didn't have much time since the Calcars were now yelling at one another. Krallix said I was his since he caught me. The pair said they had dibs on me because they came across me first, but they were also arguing with each other over who deserved me. I think it was the first time in my life someone fought over me. I'd always fanta-sized it'd be two sexy college chicks, not three aliens set on eating me.

Someone threw a punch, and a fight broke out. I worked harder. The plastic cord had cut off circulation in my hand, but my glove had thank-fully kept the cord from slicing my wrist. The cord snapped, and I jumped to my feet. I raced to grab my arm when an honest-to-god message typed out in my head.

For real.

Console.

I shook my head. Yeah, I was losing it. But of all the words, "console?" Like my brain was saying I needed to be consoled or something.

Idiot. I meant, go to the console near the door.

Ohh... console, not console (stupid English). It was like I was reading my HUD, but the message was in my head. Instead of a Heads Up Display, it was a Head Up Display. I glanced at the screen on the wall next to the closed door.

Yes, go to the console. Hurry..

Instead, I ran and grabbed my arm and then realized that I'd have to cut the emergency seal my suit formed when Krallix shot my arm off. The fight sounded like it was already dying down. I'd been hoping they'd kill each other off, but with my luck, I figured they hugged and made up and were now exchanging recipes for pot roast. But, if I could grab my blaster, I could shoot them before they noticed me, and then I could grab all my stuff and scram. Calcars were big and dumb; and more importantly, not as fast as me.

No. You're dumb. Go to the console.

I went for my blaster, and a sharp pain lit up a fire behind my eyes.

I told you to go the console, brainbag!

I holstered my blaster. Then I grabbed my helmet and slid it over my head so I wouldn't have to carry it, but I didn't seal it yet. I hustled over to the door. I needed to use the screen to open the door, anyway, so I figured I wasn't out anything to follow my insane brain.

I tapped the screen, and it lit up. It was in the Calcar language, but I could read it, no problem—it was like a two-year-old came up with the letters using fingerpaint.

I went to hit the *Open* button when my finger stuttered to the menu and tapped it. I yanked my hand away.

No, let me interface with the console.

I was starting to have a sinking suspicion that I wasn't insane and that the alien slime thriving in me was intelligent and communicating, albeit it was a lousy communicator.

I'm not lousy. Your language is tedious and boring. Now, put your fingers on the console if you want to live.

I preferred insanity.

I shakily raised my index finger and held it before the screen. Then, the oddest sensation tickled my hand and my fingers started tapping the screen without me willing them to do so. It was like I had Tourette's of the hand, and it was disturbing. "How're you doing that?"

I have access to you, thanks to you inviting me in.

My fingers flew over the menus until the screen displayed code. My fingers tapped out commands so quickly I couldn't even understand what they were typing, other than it was some type of computer code.

The door opened, and I came face to face with Krallix as my hand kept typing. He had a bloody nose which looked right at home on the face of a space orc. He seemed as surprised to see me as I was, and his features quickly morphed into a snarl. He started to walk through the door, but it whooshed closed, separating us. I stared blankly.

Krallix gave a guttural yell and pounded on the door.

Ha! I own their system.

"System? As in you took control of that door?" I asked aloud. Meanwhile, Krallix was yelling at the other two Calcars.

I own the entire ship's system. All of it.

Oh. "That's cool. Can you keep them locked out of here?"

Of course. Calcars are even dumber than you.

"Hey, that's not nice. I'm not dumb."

And yet you talk when you only need to think words to me.

"You're weirding me out, that's why. So I have time to get my stuff back?" I asked.

Yes. They can't override my control.

"Sweet!"

But they can break through the door.

"Oh, yeah. We'd better hurry." I used a knife to carefully cut open my suit's patch over my left nub of an arm. Since my helmet wasn't sealed yet, the suit didn't spit out patch-goo to auto seal the cut. I hustled to attach my arm. I kissed it the moment I felt its sensors against the nub of my bicep. "God, I missed you."

I didn't waste time before hustling to redress and secure my helmet. The moment it clicked in place, my suit attempted to seal itself. It kicked off several warnings until it finally spit out enough tar-like goop to seal my left arm. I said, "Fetch, you still with me?"

"I am. I was worried about you, Frank."

"Likewise. I'm ready to start hauling my stuff back. I'm going to open the door to this compartment. See that you open the cargo door as close as you can to speed things up."

"The Calcars are no longer an issue?" she asked.

"Not right now, but I don't know how long it'll stay that way."

"I understand. Based on your suit's tracker, I'm aligning to the door I extrapolated you're behind."

"Extrapolate away," I said and hustled to the outer door. It surprised me that this compartment didn't have an airlock since it didn't seem like the standard cargo bay like on my ship. Then again, I'd been on a whopping two spaceships— three counting the Archivist wreck—so my knowledge could be considered somewhat limited.

I opened the door and felt the suction of space tugging at me. *Fetch* was backing up against the doorway, the cargo bay opening. I turned to grab my things when the goo in my head messaged, *Console.*

I knew what it wanted this time and held my hand up to the screen next to the outer door I'd just opened. My fingers ran over menus and back into the command line screen. From there, it typed a single command and then the ship went dark.

"You shut it down?"

Worse. I gave it a malicious command.

I sensed glee. The thing inside me clearly had an ornery streak, but since Krallix and his buddies wanted to eat me, I didn't feel bad in the least.

Even with the pressure out of the compartment, I could hear them pounding on the pressurized side of the door. Noise doesn't carry far in space, but it does carry some. The Calcars were using something heavy like sledgehammers now, and the door was showing reverse dimples with every strike. The door had to be tough since it was the equivalent of an airlock, but it was taking a beating.

I hustled. I kept my mag-boots and grabbed as much as I could each trip, starting with the most important stuff. I was glad the goo had shut down the ship because it cut off the gravity in the compartment. Krallix hadn't bothered tying anything down, so everything now floated around. The first trip was the courier drone. The second trip was the data cube from the sphere, along with a handful of instruments and parts I snatched as they floated around my head. As soon as I stepped into my cargo bay, I gave everything a gentle toss so it wouldn't drift outside. On my third trip, I glanced at the inner door to see that there was now a hole, but the Calcars weren't in sight. My guess is they had to flee to get on their hab-suits since they breached their own ship.

I chuckled at the idea.

Like I said, Calcars are dumb, and I'm incredibly smart.

"If you say so," I said.

"What's that?" Fetch asked.

"Long story. I'll tell you later," I said, and reclaimed another armful of my stuff.

By my fourth trip, Krallix was back. He was

now in a hab-suit, and he was using an honest-to-god battle axe to cut through the door. A third of the door was already cut away. Another few strikes and he'd be able to fit through.

"Fetch, close the door. We gotta get out of here." I ran as quickly as I could with my stuff and leapt through the shrinking doorway. The moment I was through, I said, "Get us out of here now!"

As soon as the bay door closed, I rushed to a window and saw the three Calcars burst through the inner door and stomp toward us. Krallix stood in the outer doorway, his fists clenched, while the other two Calcars jumped from *Star Claimer* and flew to their ship.

"Uh, Fetch, did you happen to ram the engine of that other Calcar ship?" I asked.

"No, they're docked onto *Star Claimer*. If I'd struck their ship, I could've killed you. I'm not allowed to kill my captain, no matter what he does to deserve it."

I winced. "Well, fly as fast as you can because they're going to be right on our tail."

"ALLOWING that alien technoform to come into contact with your flesh was incredibly dangerous, Frank. The technoform inside you is clearly a virus, not a symbiont because symbionts would never take control of their host," Fetch said.

I asked for permission, it messaged.

"It asked permission," I said.

"It's talking to you right now, isn't it," Fetch said.

"Maybe."

"I recommend ignoring it."

"C'mon, Fetch. It might be perfectly nice and sweet."

"Based on my more extensive experience with other races and species, it's more likely vile and vicious," she said.

"So, what are you, Alien Slime in my Head? Nice and sweet or vile and vicious?" I asked.

I don't have an emotive drive, it replied.

I frowned. "That's not an answer."

It didn't message anything else.

"What the heck's an emotive drive?" I asked.

"It means it doesn't have emotions," Fetch

said. "Which means that it's purely rational and with no regard for your wellbeing."

Wrong. It's rational for me to maintain my host's health. Otherwise, I wouldn't have created smart cells specifically designed to fix you, it said. *It's also why I'm creating new smart cells to more effectively communicate with you.*

I glanced upward, like I often did when speaking to Fetch. "It just made a good point. It said it's rational to keep me alive and well." I cocked my head. "Hey, Slime. Do I just call you 'Slime,' or do you have a name?"

I am... At first, a slew of numbers appeared, and then those numbers morphed into letters. *Shrike. I am a 111.*

I smiled. "Ding, ding, chicken dinner. We have a winner. Nice to meet you, Shrike of the 111s. I'm Frank and this is Fetch, my ship's AI computer."

AI? Ha. I'd hardly call it intelligent, Shrike said.

I hissed through my teeth. "Ouch. That's not very nice."

"What did it say?" Fetch asked.

"Oh, nothing. Just some jumbled words, that's all. It struggles with my language, I think," I replied.

"You're a terrible liar."

"Maybe, but the fact stands: it did keep me from being barbequed," I said.

"Relinquishing control to an alien virus inside you to escape is the riskiest and dumbest thing you've done thus far. You're lucky it didn't decide to keep control," she said.

Needless to say, my ship wasn't overly impressed with how I escaped the Calcars.

"I could've taken control of my fingers any time I wanted." I hoped. "Besides, remember the second rule of space travel? If it's dumb but works, then it isn't dumb," I said.

"Of course I remember." She actually sounded exasperated.

I grinned. "And since it worked, that makes the idea very *un*-dumb, right?"

"If you say so, Frank. But a smart idea would've been to shoot Krallix and the other two as soon as they broke through the door, rather than allowing them to chase us. And then you would've reclaimed all our possessions from Krallix rather than leaving half of them behind."

I mumbled, "Guess that would've been kind of a smart thing to do, but I was a little preoccupied."

"We're coming up on the GOD Auditor satellite. Do I have your authority to send Jack a request for immediate aid?" Fetch asked.

"Yep, and let's hope Jack's in the mood to help us."

I hustled to the cockpit and took a seat. Peering outside, I saw a long spindly station that resembled a massive Granddaddy Longlegs. Attached to the central bulb were at least three GOD ships.

To get a head start on the Calcar bounty hunters, we'd risked taking a warpgate, which kicked off a fresh batch of errors and warnings, but if we hadn't, the Calcars, in their undamaged ship, would've caught us before we reached the nearest port of aid.

As for Krallix, I wouldn't cry if he died out there in his busted ship, but with my luck, he'd get his ship back online and fix his engine in a matter of days or weeks rather than months or years. And, if he was alive, I would guaran-damn-tee you, he'd come after me. Like I said before, if there was one thing I knew, it was Calcars knew how to hold a grudge.

We'd taken a different warpflow than planned, but it was the most direct route to the nearest GOD station. If there was one thing that *no one* in space screwed with, that was GOD. All ship crews were assigned a handler. My handler was a name I couldn't even begin to pronounce, so I called it Jack, which was fitting, since it also reminded me of a jack in the box. The first time we met, Jack gave me a fine for excessive pollution in my ship's engine emissions. I hoped it was more lenient this time.

"The request has been sent, but there's been no acknowledgement yet," she said. "And, unfortunately, I've picked up on one Calcar ship emerging from the nearest warpgate. It seems they managed to track us after all."

I rubbed my neck. "C'mon, c'mon, Jack."

"Still nothing. The Calcars will reach us in thirty minutes."

I blew out a breath. "Whatever happened to help coming to answer our distress call? You'd think someone would've been close enough to help out."

"About that... I admit I never sent a distress call," Fetch said.

"What? Why not?" My left eye twitched.

"Distress calls go on our records. In all my years of flight, I've never had a distress tag."

My jaw slackened. "I thought you were supposed to follow my orders."

"You didn't specify *when* to fire off a distress call. I intend to initiate a distress call should Jack not respond to our request," she said.

My ship had a pride problem. "How far out are the Calcars?"

"Twenty-eight minutes."

"If Jack doesn't respond in the next thirty seconds, you need to send the distress call."

"Since the nearest ship is the Calcars, a distress call now will do no good."

I gritted my teeth.

"Jack has replied. It acknowledges our request and has notified us to prepare to be boarded," Fetch said.

I glanced at an Auditor ship detaching from the station and flying toward us. I frowned. "But we don't need to be boarded. We need help against the Calcars!"

"I have provided Jack with our current predicament. It deemed that the situation did not supersede standard procedure. Jack stated that the data cube is its priority."

"Of course it is," I said drily. "At least the Calcars can't be stupid enough to attack while Jack's onboard, right?"

"We can hope."

I felt a thud as the ship docked. I grabbed the lightly colored data cube, which I'd kept by my seat next to the much smaller golden cube, and went to the airlock. Just before I opened the inner airlock, Fetch warned, "Oh, and I recommend not mentioning the technoform you're carrying. Illegal transport of an alien species can result in a fine or imprisonment."

"Oh, got it," I said to her and then thought to Shrike, *You're gonna stay quiet, right?*

I don't especially enjoy talking with you, so that's no problem, it replied.

Asshole.

I opened the inner airlock, and a bronze drone floated inside. Less than two feet tall, it had a head, torso, and two arms like humans did, but that was where any similarities ended. It had two huge, bulging, glass-like eyes and then another two smaller eyes where its ears should've been. Lines of code flickered through each of the orbs. The robot was made of some kind of translucent bronze metal. Within the metal shell of its torso, lights flickered and ran through its body like blood through a blood vessel. Each of its two hands had dozens of tendril-like fingers, which must've been an upgrade—Jack had only three fingers on each of its two hands. With the torso ending with a pointed bottom, I wouldn't have been surprised if it could spin like a top. Without legs, it looked to be only half-completed, but I guess you don't need legs when you can float.

"Salutations, Terran bioform of the Sol system," it said in a squeaky, artificial voice that sounded almost childlike. "Your request for contact was deemed legal and appropriate."

I frowned. The voice was completely different from Jack's deeper, older voice. "Wait a second. You're not Jack."

"Have no fear, Captain Frank Woods. Be assured, I am J'zchk'kv, your assigned representative of the Galactic Oversight Directorate, Extraterrestrial Public Relations Division. As we agreed upon earlier, you call me Jack. However, my housing unit is currently forty-one light years from this location. I ported into a local Auditor unit to address your request. You stated you found a data cube containing illegal instructional data on black holes. Is that correct?"

I nodded and held out the cube. "See for yourself."

One of its "hands" reached out and took the cube. Jack held the cube in front of its chest, which began displaying lights and code. It remained still, with only the lights flashing, for what felt like forever.

As I stood there and watched, I noticed my hand had come up and was reaching toward Jack. I sucked in a surprised breath and yanked it to my chest.

"The Calcars are fifteen minutes out," Fetch announced.

"We're being chased by Calcars who want to kill me. Can you help?" I asked.

Jack's pointy bottom opened, and it slid the cube inside. "Interpersonal bioformic conflict is not a registered concern."

"They already stole the cube once," I blurted, hoping that would draw its attention.

"Should they attempt to steal the data cube from this unit, they will be convicted and punished for the atrocious crime," Jack said. "Our business here is concluded."

I guffawed. "Wait, you're just going to take the cube and go? After everything I did to get it to you? Not even a thank you? Nothing?"

"You're correct. Your vessel is damaged and

emitting eight-point-sixty-two percent more pollutants than found during the last inspection. I have filed a standard emissions ticket. You have fourteen days to make payment."

"Gee, thanks," I said drily.

"This concludes our business here," it said.

"But if you let those Calcars kill me, then we'll never work together again," I said.

"That would be a fact, but unlikely. Also, another Auditor is flying out to perform a thorough inspection of the Calcar vessel. Upon initial scans, we identified fourteen laws broken because of their vessel's configuration and the contraband they carry onboard. Healthy travels, bioform."

After Jack exited, and the other airlock closed, Fetch spoke. "I saw that."

"Saw what?"

"You tried to touch Jack, but it wasn't you, was it?" she said.

I gulped. "I don't know what you're talking about."

"Yes, you do. Obviously, the virus attempted to take over, and infect Jack," she said.

I snorted. "Shrike wouldn't do that." My next words were quieter, "Would you Shrike?"

Shrike didn't answer.

I began to suspect Shrike wasn't a good angel on my shoulder after all, but a very bad angel. "Uh, maybe you can run some deeper scans on me," I mused.

"They may be painful, but I highly recommend that. Viruses tend to leave their hosts dead, and I have a vested interest in your survival," she said.

"I'd like to stay alive, too," I said.

"I also would like to have a better understanding of the technoformic virus should it attempt to infect me," she said.

I don't infect *anything; I commandeer. And I have no interest in commandeering an* artificial *technoform,* Shrike said.

I shrugged. "Shrike says it doesn't want to 'commandeer' you. Something about you being an artificial technoform, which doesn't make any sense to me. Aren't all technoforms artificial? I mean, they're technologically based, while bioforms are biologically based."

"There's nothing artificial about technology. Technoforms and bioforms are simply different domains of lifeforms, while I am a unit of artificially intelligent technology. While many ships and AI tech are casually referred to as technoforms, we are artificially generated technoforms rather than birthed by a natural race of technoforms."

"Ew, robots have sex?"

"You have a very limited view of reproduction. In fact, the vast majority of life in this universe doesn't reproduce via sex," she said.

"If you say so. What matters is that Shrike doesn't want to hurt you."

"What matters is that it's *capable* of commandeering me," Fetch said. "And that is a concept I do not like very much."

"I won't let it," I said.

"Like you wouldn't let it touch Jack?"

"I stopped it, didn't I?"

"You did, but what if it continues to spread in your body? What happens when it can take full control without your permission?" she asked.

"You'll run whatever tests you need, so we can do whatever it takes to make sure that doesn't happen."

"Your optimism is foolish."

"It's a better way of living than being a foolish pessimist." I glanced out the window. "Any update on the Calcars chasing us?"

"Yes. For the first good news in a very long time, the GOD Auditor put an engine lock on the Calcars' ship. They won't be going anywhere anytime soon. I advise we launch the courier drone to get our payment and then make haste to the next repair station," she said.

"That sounds like an excellent plan."

———

I sat in the cockpit, moping. "I can't believe Totty gave me a fifty percent penalty for sending only the databanks and not towing back the Archival ship. She saw the pictures. She knew it couldn't be towed."

"Totty will find any loophole imaginable to keep more of the payout to herself," Fetch said.

"We don't have nearly enough cards to replace all the broken crap on this ship," I griped.

"That is an accurate statement," she said. "It is unfortunate you did not find more treasure within the Dyson sphere to sell."

"I was too busy trying to stay alive." I picked up the small golden cube that fit in the palm of my hand. It was cool looking, which had to help its resale value.

You can't sell the warpgate navigator, Shrike said.

I held up the cube. "Warpgate navigator? That's what this is?"

Yes.

"Why can't I sell it?" I asked.

It's a true map of warpgates and warpflows. It's not one of those incomplete GOD maps.

I chuckled drily. "As if there are warpgates out there that someone wouldn't just stumble across."

"What is the little virus saying now?" Fetch asked.

"Shrike says this cube is a better map of the warpgates than the one everyone uses," I replied.

"That's highly unlikely."

"That's what I think, too."

"I can verify quickly enough. Place it on a data reader," Fetch ordered.

I set the cube on the reader, which was a bare black square on the horizontal part of the instrument panel. A map of the galaxy appeared on the pixelated screen that reminded me of a video game from the early 1980s. Fetch began zooming in.

"It will take some time to analyze the map," Fetch said.

Here. Let me.

"Okay, but only this one time." I brought my hand up to the keyboard interface with more than a little trepidation. My fingers began dancing over the keyboard, and the map view constantly changed. Soon, a series of warpgates were displayed. A thin line connected them, making them look like a constellation of stars.

See? That's home.

"Interesting," Fetch said. "Those warpgates

are not on any of my maps."

I shrugged. "But unmapped warpgates don't fix my ship. I think we've got to sell this."

We can use the warpgate navigator to find untold wealth—places no one's been in thousands of years, Shrike messaged. *It'll be an adventure.* Its last sentence wasn't messaged—it simply appeared in my brain as if Shrike were sitting next to me, talking. His voice was masculine and smooth. It was a little on the deeper side while also being understated. Reminded me of Jayne Cobb from *Firefly*. Since that had been my favorite show (I'd seen the reruns), I wondered if I gave it that voice, or if that was Shrike's natural voice.

I selected a voice that you'd like. I don't have a "natural" voice. Did you see me with a mouth, let alone a voice box, in your medical scans?

"Uh, no. But it's cool that you can talk to me, more or less," I said.

I waste less time talking to you in this manner than in creating visual messages in your brainpan.

"Ah, you say the sweetest things," I said. I took back the cube, collapsed back in my seat, and examined it as I considered Shrike's offer. "Untold riches sound really cool, but we can't go much of anywhere with a busted ship. We still need money first."

"You may not like the solution, but Totty is always interested in loaning cards," Fetch said.

I chortled. "I bet she's a heckuva loan shark."

"Absolutely. Though instead of paying interest, she's more likely to add extra years to your contract," she said.

I glowered. "Totty's a dick."

"Totty's a Zuddlian. The terms are inter-changeable," she said.

I considered the option for a moment before throwing up my hand. "There's an alien inside me that's I have a feeling isn't Sister Teresa. And I'm going to be eighty-seven by the time my contract runs out. The odds aren't in my favor that I'm going to live halfway through my contract, so go ahead and send a request to Totty for as much as we need. Squeeze every card you can from her."

Twenty-three seconds passed before we received Totty's reply.

"Totty has added fourteen years to your contract in exchange for fourteen thousand cards, of which you do not have to repay."

"I don't have to repay any of it?"

"She neglected to mention that, legally, adding years to your contract already counts as repayment, a repayment that allows her to deduct the full amount off her taxes."

"Ah, of course she neglected to say that," I said.

"She's also sent the next ticket."

I shook my head. "Tell her I've got to fix my ship first."

"I'll tell her, but I doubt she'll change the deadline," Fetch said.

I rubbed my eyes, stood, and walked to my bunk. "Fine, whatever. I'm going to bed. Don't wake me unless something bad happens."

———

Something bad happened four hours later.

Frank Woods, the galaxy's unluckiest space repo man, has faced his share of challenges, but nothing could prepare him for his latest assignment. His boss at the repo agency hands him a job that sounds straightforward enough: repossess an old, outdated android.

However, there's a catch—the android doesn't want to be repo'd and isn't about to go quietly.

Frank desperately needs paid, but with each attempt to catch the android, Frank faces deadly traps, high-tech trickery, and a series of bizarre challenges that test his determination.

In a battle of wits and wills, Frank may have met his match!

Get *Secondhand Singularity* today!

Secondhand Spaceman Series

The Lazarus Key

Waymaker Wars Series

Space Troopers Series

Flight of the Javelin Series

Bounty Hunter Series

Fringe Series

The Deadland Saga

Earth Under Siege: The Colliding Worlds Trilogy

Guardians of the Seven Seals

Tidy Guides (*non-fiction*)

Rachel Aukes is the award-winning author of forty novels, including *100 Days in Deadland*, which made *Suspense Magazine*'s Best of the Year list. When not writing, she can be found flying old airplanes over the Midwest countryside and catering to an exceptionally spoiled fifty-pound lapdog.

Join Rachel's spam-free newsletter to be the first to hear about new releases: www.rachelaukes.com/join

ACKNOWLEDGMENTS

With many thanks to Diane Bryant for making my stuff look good; to the Propellers for being the best damn writing group; to Brian for the hugs; to Ellie for the endless supply of doggie kisses; and to *you* for picking up this story and opening the galaxies within it.